Genovia

By Olivia Grace

A   Olivia's Room

B   Grandmère's Room

C   Mia's Room

D   Rocky's Room

E   Main Staircase

F   Throne Room

G   Ballroom

H   Billiard Room

I   Dad's Office

J   Hall of Portraits

K   Kitchens

L   Royal Dining Room

M   Royal Genovian Guards

N   Library

O   Tennis Courts

P   Stables

Q   Royal Genovian Gardens

R   Royal Genovian Academy

S   Downtown Genovia

T   Beach

U   Royal Genovian Yacht Club

Royal
Crush

From the Notebooks of a Middle School Princess

Royal Crush

Written & illustrated by

MEG CABOT

SQUARE
FISH

Feiwel & Friends ♔ New York

An imprint of Macmillan Publishing Group, LLC
175 Fifth Avenue, New York, NY 10010
mackids.com

Our books may be purchased in bulk for promotional, educational, or
business use. Please contact your local bookseller or the Macmillan Corporate
and Premium Sales Department at (800) 221-7945 ext. 5442 or by
e-mail at MacmillanSpecialMarkets@macmillan.com.

Library of Congress Control Number: 2016953575

ISBN 978-1-250-15869-7 (paperback)   ISBN 978-1-250-11151-7 (ebook)

Originally published in the United States by Feiwel and Friends
First Square Fish edition, 2018
Book designed by April Ward
Square Fish logo designed by Filomena Tuosto

1   3   5   7   9   10   8   6   4   2

AR: 5.6 / LEXILE: 880L

Monday, November 23
10:30 A.M.
Royal Genovian Academy
World Languages

So I'm going to be an aunt.

A year ago I never would have thought I'd be writing those words.

But there are lots of words I never thought I'd be writing—let alone saying—a year ago, such as:

- "I'm a princess."

- "Please have the limo brought around, Monsieur Henri, as I'm expected in half an hour to cut the ribbon at the grand opening of Genovia's first Starbucks."

- o "No, thanks, Dad, I don't care to go salmon fishing in Iceland again with you this week-end, but I appreciate your asking."

Out of all these, the fact that I'm going to be an aunt (especially at age thirteen, which I'll be exactly five days from today) seems the weirdest.

Even weirder is that I'm going to be an aunt to royal twins. That's the part everyone in the whole world is talking about.

Seriously. You can't go online without seeing a post from some celebrity—from Kim Kardashian to the president—guessing what sex Princess Mia of Genovia's babies are going to be, or what she and her husband, Michael, are going to call them.

It's so weird to me that total strangers care so much about something that has nothing to do with them. Most of them don't even live in Genovia!

And okay, I get that royal twins aren't born every day. But professional bookies in Las Vegas have begun taking bets on the babies' sexes, names, and birthday!

They're giving two-to-one odds that both babies will be girls, their names will be Clarisse and Mignonette, and they'll be born on December 3.

It's not like Mia and Michael are doing anything to encourage this craziness. The opposite, in fact: They haven't posted the twins' sonograms on their Facebook pages (they don't even have Facebook pages—though there's a page for the Palace of Genovia, where you can find out what time it's open to the public for tours).

They haven't even told anyone in the *family* what the babies' sexes (or names) are! All they've told us is the due date (it's in two weeks).

Which made Grandmère huff, "What good does *that* do us? How can I tell Tiffany's what initials to monogram on the miniature gold scepters I've ordered if I don't even know the babies' names? I understand why you wouldn't want the rest of the world to know, Amelia, but I don't see how telling *me* the babies' names could hurt."

Except that telling Grandmère the babies' names *could* hurt. Every time Mia has suggested a name in front of our grandmother, Grandmère has said, "Oh, no, you can't possibly name either of the babies *that*. There was a girl in my class called that, and she used to:

- chew with her mouth open.

- show off her double-jointed legs at recess.

- brag about how many Chanel handbags she owned.

"You simply can't burden a child with *that* name."

This happened so many times that Mia's blood pressure began to rise . . . so much so that the royal obstetrician had to put her on bed rest out of fear for the babies' health. The doctor wouldn't allow her to do any of her royal duties *or* have any visitors who might cause her stress. . . .

This turned out to include Grandmère.

You can imagine how unhappy this made some people (mainly Grandmère).

But it worked. Mia's blood pressure is almost down to normal (although the doctor still won't let her get out of bed).

And, as an added bonus, I have now seen almost every teen movie ever made! Because I'm one of the people who was judged low-stress enough to visit Mia, and she decided my entertainment education has been sadly neglected, so we've been watching nonviolent movies together in her room almost every day.

Anyway, I guess given all of the above, I shouldn't have been too surprised just now when I was Skyping with my best friend, Nishi, and all she could talk about was my sister and the babies.

What *did* surprise me was the incredibly rude way she brought it up:

"I saw a photo of your sister last night on Rate the Royals," Nishi said.

"How?" I asked. "She's on full bed rest. She hasn't been anywhere."

"I think they got a picture of her through one of the palace windows with a telephoto lens. I was shocked she's gotten so fat. One of those babies *has* to be a boy."

"*Excuse* me?"

I couldn't believe what I was hearing. Nishi lives in America, so if we want to talk, we have to call each other, FaceTime, or Skype.

I know I shouldn't have been Skyping during World Languages, and that I should have been practicing my German instead.

But in my defense, everyone had their headphones on, including Madame Chi, so it wasn't like anyone was going to hear me, and I'd already finished all my German homework.

"I'm just saying," Nishi went on, oblivious to how mad I was at her for calling my sister fat. "Your sister is as big as a house! She's too huge to be having two girls. My mom says when a pregnant woman is that big, it's got to be boys. Or a boy and a girl, at least."

Obviously I had no choice but to do what I did next. It was a matter of family pride.

"You're wrong," I said, feeling my che

"You are so wrong, I will *bet* you that you'

"What?" Nishi sounded confused. *"Bet*

want to *bet* me that I'm wrong?"

"Yes," I said.

I get why Nishi was surprised. It's conside

"poor form" for royals to gamble. The last time Nish

had been to Genovia to visit—over the summer—

one of my cousins (I have so many cousins, even I

can't keep all of them straight) had been caught in a

horse-race gambling scandal, and Grandmère had

gone on and on about how he'd disgraced the family,

and what were we going to do, but that it was only to

be expected considering the fact that he came from

the Italian side of the family, and that side of the

family is known for acting without thinking first, et

cetera.

And now here I was not only gambling but gam-

bling on the sexes of my sister's unborn twins!

But in my defense, everyone was doing it. I'd even

overheard Lars, my sister's bodyguard, make a bet

lyguard, that the babies would

v sister would name one of

usband, and the other

which Serena had had

ie bet, then told Lars that

anted his money in American

s.

bet you anything you want that both

are girls," I said to Nishi.

Nishi looked even more surprised. She was in her bedroom back in New Jersey. Because of the time difference between Genovia and America, she hadn't yet left for school. The only reason she was up so early was to chat with me.

"Anything I want?" she asked, raising her eyebrows.

"Sure," I said, not thinking of the consequences (which, I have to say, is very rare for me. Normally, I am much more levelheaded, being a Sagittarius). "You name it."

"Great!" Nishi said. "Then if I'm right and at

least one of the babies is a boy, I want four photos of my crush, Prince Khalil."

That's when I realized I'd made a really big mistake. REALLY big. "Wait. What?"

"You heard me," Nishi said. "I want four photos, taken by you, of Prince Khalil. I want two of him smiling, one of him looking serious—because you know how cute he looks when he gets all serious about something and those eyebrows of his get all squinchy in the middle—and one of him smiling in front of a sunset, preferably without a shirt on."

"But . . . but . . ." I could not believe what I had just gotten myself into. "That's—"

"That's what?" Nishi demanded. "You said anything I want, and that's what I want."

"But why?" I burst out, then realized I'd spoken too loudly when several people sitting near me in the language lab—including another one of my cousins, Lady Luisa Ferrari—turned to stare at me, wondering what I was doing, since it definitely wasn't speaking German. I hunched my shoulders to cover my computer screen, and also lowered my voice. "Why, Nishi?" I whispered. "Why do you want photos of Prince Khalil? I thought you liked some boy in your English class—Dylan or something?"

"I do," Nishi said. "But I can like more than one boy at a time, can't I? We're in the seventh grade, Olivia, not college. We're *supposed* to like a lot of different boys at a time."

I sighed, realizing that Nishi had gotten even more boy crazy than I thought since the last time I'd seen her.

Not that there's anything wrong with being boy—or girl—crazy. This is something that happens to people. I mean, I get it: Everyone grows and changes as they get older—they can't help it. Look at me: I've grown *two whole inches* since I last saw Nishi. My riding habit barely fits anymore.

We'd planned to see each other again soon—at my sister's coronation, as a matter of fact. Since Dad gave up ruling in order to spend more time with me (he missed out on most of my crucial formative years), Mia has to take over the throne.

But then the coronation got postponed, because the royal physicians didn't want Mia risking her or the babies' health by having her stand for a huge long ceremony in the throne room, which doesn't have air-conditioning. It's too old.

(This was not the official explanation from the palace. They decided to say that the coronation would be held next December 31, so that they could save expenses by combining the annual New Year's fireworks with the fireworks for Mia's coronation. But really they knew the babies would have been born by then, the weather would be cooler, and they could cram more people into the throne room without them dying of heat prostration.)

So we postponed Nishi's next visit until my birthday ball this weekend.

But now Nishi's parents won't let her come because she's getting a D in English—which I don't understand, since English is our native language.

Nishi says it's because of Dylan, whose cute lips distract her, making it very difficult for her to pay attention.

So you can see why I found it hard to believe she suddenly wanted photos of Prince Khalil—without a shirt on—if she won our bet.

"How am I even supposed to do that, Nishi? How am I supposed to get a photo of Prince Khalil with no shirt on, smiling in front of a sunset?"

"I don't know," Nishi said. "That's not my problem. You're the one who made the bet. Can't you just ask him to stand in front of a sunset without a shirt on and smile? I thought you two were friends . . . unless—wait." Nishi's eyes widened. "Olivia, do *you* like him?"

"What?" I cried. "No! Of course not. What are you even talking about?"

"Well," she said, "you two danced at your sister's wedding—"

"Yeah," I said. "But it's not like we were ever *going out* or anything. We were only ever friends."

"*Were?*" Nishi echoed. "You aren't friends anymore?"

"Yes," I said. "I mean, no. I mean . . . I don't know. It's hard to tell sometimes with boys."

"Ha!" Nishi let out a sarcastic laugh. "You're telling me. Boys are an enigma wrapped in a mystery."

She wasn't kidding.

And it was especially true in the case of Prince Khalil. He had come over to visit a couple of times during the summer, and we'd played floating table tennis in the pool and talked about autotomy (the ability of lizards to drop their tails when threatened by a predator) and movies and stuff.

And then suddenly I didn't see him at all. He'd texted that he had to "go home," and that was it.

It wasn't until school started up again that I saw him in class, and then he was just like, "Hi," but he didn't smile or ask how Carlos, my pet iguana, was doing or anything.

It wasn't like he was mean, but something had changed. The connection I thought we'd felt when we'd talked about Carlos and danced together at Mia's wedding or played floating table tennis over the summer was gone, and all that was left was just . . . nothing.

So now I don't know what's going on.

"Well, whatever," I said to Nishi. "It isn't going to matter, because I'm going to win this bet anyway. And when I win, you're going to send me a big jar of peanut butter, because we can't get that here in Genovia."

Nishi gasped. "What? Why not?"

"I don't know," I said with a shrug. "We have Nutella instead."

"Nutella is better than peanut butter," Nishi said. "But fine, it's a bet."

I would have asked her to tell me what other stuff people were saying about my sister, but Madame Alain had just come on over the intercom with an important announcement, and I needed to log off and listen.

It was probably just as well, since anything else Nishi told me would only have made me mad. People say the stupidest things, especially about royals.

I should have known when Madame Alain said she had an important announcement that it wasn't going to be good news.

I don't know why I thought it was going to be something nice, like that we were all going to get to go home early because the new baby princesses of Genovia had been born (except that I had already made my dad promise that if Mia went into labor while I was in school, I'd get pulled out of class immediately and brought to the hospital so that I could be one of the first people to meet the babies, and they would imprint upon me like baby ducks and then follow me everywhere).

But no. The announcement was nothing like that.

Instead it was:

"Your Royal Majesties, Highnesses, Graces, lords, ladies, and gentlemen, I'm sorry to inform you that I have only received twenty-seven permission slips for this week's trip to the Royal School Winter Games in Stockerdörfl," Madame Alain said after some of the hissing, screeching, and feedback had died down over the intercom.

The Royal Genovian Academy is a very fancy school, with extremely high tuition fees (except for the two hundred or so refugee children who had recently been admitted—they are allowed to attend tuition-free), but it's also housed in a building that was constructed before sound systems (or electricity) were invented, so it has a lot of technical problems.

"As you know, unless I receive at least another

thirty permission slips from those of you who signed up for the trip last week, the Royal Genovian Academy's participation in this year's Royal School Winter Games will be canceled due to lack of interest."

Of course as soon as he heard the name of his hometown mentioned, Prince Gunther Lapsburg von Stuben of Stockerdörfl stood up and gave a fist pump, causing a few of the younger girls in the language lab to squeal. (Prince Gunther is considered extremely good-looking, for a seventh grader.)

This annoyed my cousin Lady Luisa, who flashed the girls a dirty look. She and Prince Gunther have been going out since June, even though all "going out" means in the seventh grade at the Royal Genovian Academy is holding hands. Anything more than that would be a violation of the school's "honor code." If they get caught, the head of the school, Madame Alain, will probably expel them, and they'll have no choice but to attend The Royal Academy in Switzerland, or worse—to Luisa, anyway—Genovian public school.

Luisa grabbed Prince Gunther by the arm and tugged him back into his seat. He looked confused, not knowing—as usual—what he'd done to offend her.

"It's *canceled*," Luisa hissed into Prince Gunther's ear. "She just said our trip to the Games is going to be *canceled*. Why are you so excited?"

Prince Gunther looked as hurt as if someone had punched him in the gut. "Canceled? No!"

Luisa rolled her eyes. Except for the fact that the Games meant getting out of class for a few days, no one at the Royal Genovian Academy cared very much about them . . . no one except for Prince Gunther.

"I know how much of a blow this might be to some of you," Madame Alain went on over the intercom, almost as if she'd seen Prince Gunther's look of sadness. "I am extremely disappointed that so many of our royals seem to be lacking in the kind of pride for our school that I have come to expect from students at the Royal Genovian Academy.

"But it is not simply that we don't have enough permission slips. This illness that so many of you are referring to as La Grippe—when it is, in fact, merely a little cold—has struck down many of our finest athletes. Princess Charlotte on our cross-country ski team. The Contessa Gerante on the girls' hockey team. Even Lady Marguerite is apparently too ill to work a camera and take photos for the school yearbook, which I find somewhat hard to believe. But there it is."

I raised my eyebrows at this. Lady Marguerite is another one of my cousins. I knew she hadn't been feeling well, but I also knew how much she'd been looking forward to going on this school trip. (She'd wanted to get out of a test we were having in Algebra on Friday.)

She must have actually been feeling sick.

La Grippe is a particularly nasty flu that has been going around our school as well as up and down the Mediterranean coast. It is pronounced *La Greep* but sounds even nastier when someone like Grandmère or Madame Alain says it, because they both roll their *r*'s and pronounce the letter *i* like *ee*, so it comes out sounding like *La Grrreeeeeeep.*

Yuck!

Half the student population of the Royal Genovian Academy seems to have come down with La Grippe, and so has the faculty.

It's gotten so bad, it's started affecting other things at school besides field trips to the Alps:

"In addition," Madame Alain went on, "because my administrative assistant, Monsieur Gerard, was too ill to come to work last week, we were unable to make your seating assignments for lunch today. Therefore, you may sit wherever you like. Thank you, and remember: Manners matter!"

Though the walls at the RGA are nearly three feet thick, I could hear cheering from the high school classrooms all the way down to the kindergarten (and that was across the courtyard, in another building). Normally, seating for lunch at the Royal Genovian Academy is assigned (like at a wedding), so that we don't form into "friend groups."

Madame Alain *hates* friend groups. She thinks an important part of our training to be "leaders of tomorrow" is developing the ability to make polite conversation with *anyone*—from the lowliest sixth grader to the tallest senior—and she does that by assigning seats and forcing us to eat lunch with different people every day.

But today we were going to be able to sit anywhere we wanted.

While I felt sorry for Madame Alain's administrative assistant, this was definitely an unexpected benefit of La Grippe.

So I guess the news wasn't *all* bad . . . at least, not to me. Some people, however, were pretty upset by it.

"Madame Chi," Prince Gunther cried, leaping to his feet. "If replacements can be found for those suffering with La Grippe, could we not still go to Stockerdörfl on Wednesday?"

Madame Chi, sitting at the front of the language lab, looked as if she might have been coming down with La Grippe herself. Rubbing her temples with her fingers, she sighed so heavily that a curl that had escaped from the tight bun in which she always wore her hair fluttered up into the air.

"Well, Your Highness, I don't know . . . it's terribly late. But I suppose you could always ask."

Prince Gunther spun around to face our class.

"Come on, everyone!" he cried. "I know you can do better than this! Show some school pride! Get your permission slips to your parents and get them signed. We *have* to go to the Games. And we have to win! We have to beat TRAIS!"

TRAIS stands for The Royal Academy in Switzerland, against whom the Royal Genovian Academy competes every year at the Royal School Winter Games, a kind of Olympics for all the royal schools in Europe. (The Royal Academy in Switzerland swept most of the medals last year. I understand that they even won the spirit contest, showing better sportsmanship than the RGA by wearing matching tracksuits and chanting, "Go team, go, TRAIS, TRAIS, TRAIS!" at each event. This would be unthinkable to any student at the RGA.)

This year the Games are taking place in Prince Gunther's Austrian village of Stockerdörfl, just a short—well, okay, fourteen-hour—train ride from Genovia. Prince Gunther's parents, Prince Hans and Princess Anna-Katerina Lapsburg von Stuben, are going to hand out the medals at the closing ceremonies.

So I guess I can see why Prince Gunther is so excited. If the Games were being hosted in Genovia, with my family handing out medals, I might have been more enthusiastic.

But despite Prince Gunther's impassioned speech about beating TRAIS, everyone (except me) whipped out their cell phones and began pressing buttons . . . not to ask their parents to sign and send over their permission slips, but to text one another about where to sit for lunch.

I think Madame Alain is right: the RGA really does have zero school spirit.

And I'm afraid that might include me. I've carefully refrained from mentioning anything about the Games to my dad, stepmom, Grandmère, or Mia. Why would I want to go to some dumb royal kids' competition when my sister is due to have royal twins at ANY MOMENT? Especially since new-borns can't really see all that well (according to my sister's birthing books). They become accustomed to those closest to them during those all-important first few days in their life by the sound of their voices.

No way am I leaving Genovia and missing out on that.

Monday, November 23
1:15 P.M.
Royal Genovian Academy
Lunch

Oh dear.

Right after the bell rang for lunch, as I yelled at Princess Komiko to please wait for me because I'd forgotten my backpack, then whirled around to get it, I nearly smacked right into Prince Khalil.

I've gotten much more graceful (in my opinion) than last year when Mademoiselle Justine, RGA's dance instructor, despaired of me ever learning to do a proper Genovian folk dance.

But I still occasionally bump into things.

And today what I bumped into was Prince Khalil Rashid bin Zayed Faisal.

He was super nice about it, though, bending over to help me pick up all the things that had scattered out of my backpack and pretending like I hadn't just made a total idiot out of myself.

He even asked—looking at me with the same thoughtful, sad expression he's been wearing on his face ever since returning to school at the beginning of the new semester—"Are you all right, Princess Olivia?"

"Me?" I squeaked as I gathered up all the German flashcards I'd made for myself so I could remember my vocabulary words. *"I'm* fine. What about *you?"*

He smiled. It was the first time I'd seen him smile all semester, practically, and the look of it made my heart sing.

There was still something a bit sad in his smile, though, and that made me feel sad, too.

"I'm fine also," he said. "You seem very excited."

"Oh," I said. "I *am* excited!"

"About the Royal School Winter Games?"

"What? No!" I made a face. "About the fact that we get to sit wherever we want at lunch today!"

His smile grew confused. "Wait . . . so you're not going to the Games?"

"Oh, goodness, no," I said. Then I noticed that his smile had disappeared altogether, and he was regarding me with a look that seemed more troubled than ever. "What I mean is . . ." What had I said wrong? Was Prince Khalil upset with my lack of school spirit? "I can't. I have to stay in Genovia until my sister's babies are born. I've got to be here for the birth. I'm going to be an aunt, you know."

His dark eyebrows, which he'd furrowed when I'd said I wasn't going to the Games, relaxed after I explained why.

"Oh," he said. "That makes sense."

"Does it?" I laughed a little nervously. I was still mortified from having crashed into him, but also a little freaked out that we were the only two people left in the language lab. It had been one thing to be alone with him back when we'd been friends and could talk so easily about our mutual love of iguanas.

It was quite another to be alone with him now that this strange distance had grown between us.

"I'm afraid people are going to call me a dork when they find out," I said, climbing to my feet, my backpack secured. "But I'd rather stay home with my sister and her new babies—when she has them—than go skiing in the Alps." I smiled at him in a fashion that was probably 100 percent dorky.

He didn't smile back, though. In fact, he climbed to his own feet, then said, very seriously, "I don't think there's anything weird about wanting to stay close to your family. And I'd never think you were a dork, Olivia. In fact, just the opposite. You'll see. . . ."

But instead of telling me what it was I was going to see, he turned and left. He just shouldered his own backpack, turned around, and left the language lab.

And that was it. That was the end of our conversation.

I don't want to sound sexist or anything—my sister says making prejudicial remarks about people based on their gender is called sexism—but boys can be really weird sometimes.

(Although I guess girls can be, too.)

Now I better put my pen down, because it's rude to write in your journal when you're supposed to be eating lunch with someone. (I asked Princess Komiko to sit next to me, after all, and she has to be wondering what I've been writing about this whole time instead of talking to her over our salades Niçoises.)

Monday, November 23
5:45 P.M.
Royal Genovian Bedroom

I know I should be concentrating on more important things—for instance, tonight we're having a banquet in honor of volunteer trainers of Hearing Dogs for Deaf People, and I'm giving each of the volunteers the Bronze Medal of Appreciation for Genovian Generosity.

But all I can think about is how Prince Khalil said I'm the opposite of a dork, and that I'd see. See what? I haven't seen anything yet, except that he avoided me the whole rest of the day (no big change from any other day).

I guess I must have been really distracted by this since at high tea with Grandmère in the Royal Genovian Gardens, she said, "Olivia, I can't imagine what's wrong with you today, but this is the third time I've had to ask you to pass the clotted cream. Please pay attention. If I were a dignitary visiting from a foreign land, you could have caused an international incident by ignoring me so rudely."

"Oh, I'm so sorry, Grandmère," I said, and passed the clotted cream. "I'm just having a hard time concentrating, I guess."

"Ah," Grandmère said. "Well, yes, we're all feeling a little down about the fact that, once again, your sister cannot join us at the tea table. But fortunately we have your father here for once, so let us bask in the radiance of his manly presence."

"Mother," Dad said, turning the page of the newspaper he was reading, "please. All I said was that I'd join you for an espresso."

"Which is not, nor has it ever been, tea, but we will take what we can get. Shall we ask Olivia why it is that she's so out of sorts, or would you prefer to read about the stock market, Phillipe?"

Dad lowered the newspaper. "What is bothering you, Olivia?"

"It's just," I said, "that Prince Khalil used to like me, but then he went away for the summer, and ever since he came back, he's seemed really down, and today he said he thinks I'm the opposite of a dork, and that I'd see. But he didn't say what the opposite of a dork is, or what it is I'm going to see. And anyway, I thought being a dork was a good thing. Mia's always said so."

"Good heavens," Grandmère said, adding jam to the cream on her scone. "Phillipe, are you listening to this?"

"Yes." Dad had stuck his face back into the newspaper. "I think you should ignore him, Olivia. Ignore all boys."

"Phillipe, you aren't even paying attention. The child is speaking of Prince Khalil of Qalif. Prince

Khalil of the *Zayed Faisals* of Qalif." Grandmère poked her butter knife at Dad's newspaper.

Dad lowered the newspaper. "Olivia," he said, "I not only want you to ignore that particular boy, I want you to stay away from him. Period."

"What?" I dropped the piece of cake I'd been about to eat. Snowball, my puppy, found it beneath my chair and gobbled it up. "But Dad, what are you talking about? Prince Khalil and I are friends." At least, we used to be. "Remember, he used to come over all the time this summer—"

"Yes, honestly, Phillipe." Grandmère poured herself some more tea. "It isn't the boy's fault that his uncle has turned into a megalomaniac who is purposely trying to destroy his own country."

"What?" I cried again.

"That's where your Prince Khalil went this summer when he seemed to disappear," Grandmère explained. "Back to his own country with his parents, who were doubtless trying to talk sense into the boy's uncle, the supreme leader of Qalif. But the man wouldn't listen, preferring to plunge his kingdom into civil war than save his own people. So poor Khalil and his parents had no choice but to smuggle out whatever of their meager belongings they could salvage, and return here. Now your sweet Khalil is a prince without a country."

"Mother," Dad said, "you're making the boy sound like the hero of a romance novel."

"I'm not making him *sound* like anything," Grandmère declared. "I'm only stating the facts as they are written—some of them in that very newspaper you are holding, Phillipe."

She pointed at it, and I couldn't help noticing one of the headlines between Dad's fingers:

CIVIL WAR IN QALIF

"Oh no," I cried, dropping another piece of cake. This time I

didn't notice what happened to it, whether Snowball ate it or what.

Dad saw what I was looking at, then quickly tucked the paper away so I couldn't see the headline anymore.

"Don't worry about Prince Khalil, Olivia," Dad said. "He and his parents are quite safe here in Genovia. Your sister and I are seeing to that. There's no need for you to involve yourself in his difficulties."

"How can she not involve herself in the boy's difficulties?" Grandmère asked. "She is his friend. And then you tell her—quite cruelly, I might add—to stay away from him."

"Mother," Dad said with a sigh. "Of course I didn't mean for her to stay away from him completely as if he were some sort of leper. I only meant—"

"What did you mean, Phillipe? Because it sounded to me like you meant stay away from him completely. Whereas if I were the one giving Olivia advice, I might say it would be a good idea for her to be a little extra kind to him during this horrible time—even if he might seem a little . . . odd, as he was today."

"Extra kind?" I wrinkled my nose. "Like how?" Luisa was extra kind to Prince Gunther in school—holding his hand between classes, texting him heart emojis, and stuff like that—but those were the sorts of things I definitely did not want to do with Prince Khalil, or he might get the idea that I was in love with him, or something.

"Well, by paying special attention to him," Grandmère said. "People who have experienced profound loss, as your Prince Khalil has, can be known to suffer from low self-esteem. It's likely that because he's lost everything, he feels that he is not worthy of you anymore . . . especially considering what a beautiful flower you are blossoming into—"

"Mother! *Please*." Dad threw down his newspaper and stood up. "This is precisely what I was talking about. Stop filling her head with such melodramatic nonsense."

"I recall a certain prince who did a good deal of

pining after a beautiful woman he thought *he* wasn't worthy enough to have," Grandmère said with a sniff. "No one accused *him* of being melodramatic."

Dad rolled his eyes and stomped back into the palace, saying he had work to do . . . which was funny, since he's officially retired.

But I don't care what he thinks. I'm going to take Grandmère's advice and try to do something nice for Prince Khalil. That's what royals do best—perform random acts of kindness for others less fortunate than themselves.

Tuesday, November 24
6:15 A.M.
Royal Genovian Bedroom

It's official:

I'm an aunt!

The twins were born this morning at 3:22 and 3:26 A.M., respectively—which was quite a surprise. When we were having dinner last night (with the volunteer trainers of Hearing Dogs for Deaf People), Mia didn't show the slightest sign of going into labor. In fact, she had two helpings of blancmange.

(She wasn't even supposed to be out of bed, but she can't resist blancmange.)

I had no idea anything out of the ordinary was going on until just now, when my wardrobe consultant, Francesca, burst into my room.

"Your Highness!" Francesca cried, her eyes glittering madly as she switched on the lights. "It's happened! The babies—they are here!"

"Why didn't anyone wake me up sooner?" I leaped out of bed.

Instead of feeling excited, the way I thought I would when the babies were born, I felt terrible.

First of all, my sister had gone through labor and delivery without me! I know from having watched many hours of *Call the Midwife*—one of my sister's favorite shows—and of course so many Lifetime movies this summer that having a baby is no joke.

"Prince Michael didn't want the press tipped off as to what was happening," Francesca explained as she helped me into my robe. "You've seen all the paparazzi waiting outside the palace?"

I nodded. Since they have no idea when the babies are due, they have been lurking around, hoping to get the first scoop as to the twins' sexes and names and weights and whatnot, so they can tell the world.

"They follow any car that leaves the front gates," Francesca reminded me. "So Prince Michael felt the fewer cars heading from the palace to the hospital, the better. In fact, he and the princess took one of the Royal Genovian Guard's personal cars to the hospital, hoping to throw the press off the scent—"

"Of course."

Trick the Paparazzi is a game we play almost daily. It's the only way to have any sort of peace and quiet when you're a royal.

"But now that the babies are born, and both they and your sister are doing well, Prince Michael says it's fine for everyone to come visit. So we've got to find you something absolutely *exquisite* to wear!"

According to Francesca, there isn't any problem in life—or at least royal life—that can't be solved by wearing something "absolutely exquisite."

That's why as soon as a sleepy Paolo finishes styling my hair, I'll be wearing a Genovian-blue satin dress (with matching blue ballet flats, white lace tights, and a white cardigan) to the hospital.

It's kind of weird that I have to have my hair and wardrobe professionally styled just to go to the hospital to see my sister and her new babies.

But that's royal life, I guess.

It wasn't until Paolo was putting the last drop of Moroccan oil on my hair that I thought to ask, "Oh, what are they? The babies, I mean? Two girls, right?"

That's when I found out the news that caused the bottom to drop out of my world, and the second reason I feel so terrible:

"Oh, Principessa," Paolo said. "Your sister, she has had one of each! A little girl and a little boy! It is a joyous day, no?"

Uh, no. Joyous for everyone else, maybe.

But not for me.

Tuesday, November 24
11:05 A.M.
Royal Genovian Academy
World Languages

Wow. *Wow.*

I know Grandmère would want me to think of something more descriptive to say than "Wow" about the two newest members of my family.

But "Wow" is all I can come up with at the moment.

On *Call the Midwife*, when women have babies, they come out looking all adorably cute and smiley (if a bit slimy).

But when I peeked over the side of the blankets Mia and Michael were holding, I didn't see anything cute. All I saw was a tiny, red-faced, screaming little monster.

I know. I'm sorry. I know I'm not supposed to say this. Especially about a member of the royal family . . . especially not *my* family.

And I never would say it out loud. I would only write it here, which is what journals are for: expressing your innermost thoughts and feelings.

But believe me, I wasn't the only one who thought this.

"Oh . . . *my.*"

Grandmère had to take her diamond-framed eyeglasses out of the pocket of her mink sports vest to give her first great-grandchildren a second

look before she could even bring herself to speak.

"Aren't they just beautiful?" Mia cooed from her hospital bed, cradling her daughter.

"Er, yes," Grandmère said, having to raise her voice to be heard over the screaming of the newest heirs to the throne. "I suppose *beautiful* is one word that could be used to describe them. . . ."

"The most beautiful babies in the world," Michael agreed, staring, googly-eyed, down at his angrily shrieking son.

I guess when you're a parent—if you're a good one—you love your kids no matter what. You love them so much, you don't even notice when they look (in Rocky's words) "like sunburned praying mantises."

(Fortunately he only said this in the car on our way to school, not in the hospital room with Mia and her mom and Dad and Michael and the nurses and the royal photographer all standing there.)

"And what have you decided to name these, er, beautiful creatures?" Grandmère screamed over all the crying.

"Oh, we haven't decided yet," Mia said, gazing adoringly down into her baby's roaring little face.

"You . . . haven't . . . decided . . . yet?" Grandmère repeated.

"No," Mia said. "They have such amazing little personalities, don't they, Michael?"

"Yes," Michael said. "They do."

When she smiled over the blue bundle that Michael was holding, I could have sworn that the little face in that bundle stopped howling for a minute and smiled back—even though I know from my extensive reading about babies (in preparation for when I might have to babysit my niece and nephew, even though of course they'll have a full-time nanny) that newborns don't smile—at least on purpose—for a few weeks after birth.

"None of the names we picked out for them fit," Mia went on. "We're going to need to spend more time with them before we decide which names do. Aren't we?" she asked the shrieking baby in her arms. "Aren't we, my little precious one?"

I guess the baby said yes, because that's what Mia and Michael have decided to do.

In the hospital room, Rocky and Grandmère and I all said we thought this was a really great idea.

But later, in the limo on the way back to school, Rocky grumbled, "I think the names I suggested— Princess Ninja Quest and Prince Star Fighter—were perfect. I don't know why Mia and Michael didn't like them."

Grandmère said she didn't know why Mia and Michael didn't like the names she suggested, either.

"What is so wrong with Clarisse?" she asked. "Or Phillipe? So simple. So elegant. Why can't they name the babies Clarisse and Phillipe and be done with it?"

"I know, Grandmère," I said, patting her on the

shoulder, because I could tell she was upset. "I'm sure they'll use your suggestions as middle names, at least."

"Middle names!" Grandmère sniffed. "I'm tired of having my perfectly good first name always used as a *middle* name!"

Meanwhile, Rocky was concerned about something else. "What about the babies' heads, Grandmère? Will they stay that pointy forever?"

You could tell from his voice that he thought it might be cool if they did.

"Don't be absurd. They should begin to look more normal in a few days. Although, come to think of it, Phillipe took considerably longer. But he was a particularly hideous baby—and huge. Ten pounds. Your grandfather gave me this sapphire ring when he was born to thank me. Isn't it lovely?"

Rocky and I agreed that the ring was lovely. "And big, too."

"Of course it's big," Grandmère said. "One carat for every pound your father weighed at birth.

Although, truthfully, thanks to the advent of laughing gas, I didn't feel a thing. When I had your father, the nurse strapped the mask onto me, handed me a copy of *Vogue*, and ten minutes later, out popped the new heir to the throne of Genovia."

Honestly, I've heard more about childbirth today than I've ever cared to. I'm happy I'm an aunt because that means I'll get to experience babies without having to have one myself, which is fine by me for now.

"Still, it's extraordinary how many attractive people there are in the world who started out life as repulsively ugly babies," Grandmère went on. "In my experience, the more beautiful the child, the uglier the adult he or she grows up to be—not necessarily on the outside, of course. More often on the inside."

This is an interesting theory. I'm pretty sure it applies to my cousin Lady Luisa Ferrari, who is the most beautiful girl in my whole school (in her own opinion, anyway).

But she's also one of the most annoying people

I've ever met (though I've been trying to teach her not to be).

Take right now, for instance. She sits behind me in World Languages and won't stop bombarding me with notes.

Your birthday ball this weekend better not be canceled because of those dumb babies! My grandmother got me a genuine red floor-length ball gown by Claudio, and Prince Gunther will be wearing a matching red tie and cummerbund. So I don't want them to go to waste!

And what are the twins' names? I know you know!

Lady Luisa Ferrari

This just bounced into my lap. (Since we're not allowed to use our cell phones during class, Luisa didn't want to risk detention by texting me. Passing notes was far less risky.)

I turned in my seat to glare at her. Luisa glared right back, then mouthed, *Tell me!*

Everyone in school—everyone in the *whole world*,

practically—knows that the royal twins have been born and what sexes they are.

It hasn't yet been officially announced that Michael and Mia have no idea what to call them. Rocky and I have been sworn to secrecy.

I turned Luisa's note over and began writing on the back of it:

Yes, of course we're still having the ball—why wouldn't we?

For my thirteenth birthday, my family is throwing me a gigantic ball. This is apparently what happens when you're a princess and you turn thirteen.

Personally, I would rather have had a pool party. But Grandmère said princesses don't have pool parties (except for less formal occasions).

So a ball is what I'm getting. Everyone in my whole school, practically, is invited, including Prince Khalil.

He RSVP'd yes, but I'm almost 100 percent sure he isn't going to ask me to dance. Which is fine. It really is. I swear.

I continued writing:

But even if my ball did get canceled, I don't see why you and Prince Gunther wouldn't be able to wear your Claudio creations somewhere else—unless you two break up due to one of your fights or something.

And no, I won't tell you the twins' names. You'll have to wait until the official announcement, like everyone else.

Princess Olivia

Then I tossed the note back to her, after first making sure that Monsieur Chaudhary (he is subbing for Madame Chi, who is out sick today with La Grippe) wasn't looking.

Luisa caught the note, read it, turned very red in the face, and then scribbled furiously on a new slip of paper,

Of course we could wear our Claudios somewhere else. We just don't happen to have any more balls on our schedule at the moment.

And what do you mean. "one of our fights"? Prince Gunther and I never fight!!! We are totally and completely in love in a way that you are too immature to understand.

And get over yourself. Your Royal Highness. I'm FAMILY. And that means I should find out the names of the royal babies early (they're my RELATIVES).

You never want to have fun: Stop being such a stick-in-the-mud. or I'm going to start calling you by a new nickname—STICK!

Lady Luisa Ferrari

I pressed my lips together. *Stick?* Was she kidding? That was even worse than the nickname she used to call me, *Kee-yow* (because I once mispronounced the word *ciao*. How was I supposed to know it was pronounced *chow* and not *kee-yow*?).

Of all my cousins—and when you're royal, people will come up with the slightest excuse to go on those ancestry Web sites to prove that they're related to you, so I have hundreds, if not thousands—Lady Luisa Ferrari is the worst.

She is also the snobbiest, the biggest liar, and the

most dramatic. *She's* calling *me* immature? Talk about immature! She and Prince Gunther fight *all the time*!

They break up about twice a week, usually for the dumbest reasons imaginable, like because Prince Gunther didn't text Luisa back within five seconds of her texting him, or because Prince Gunther did something Luisa considers "immature" (something she calls me all the time, too).

But I happen to know (because Grandmère told me) that everyone grows and matures at their own rate.

And no one should be made to feel inferior for not maturing at the same rate as their peers, the way Luisa tries to make me (and Prince Gunther) feel!

So sometimes when Luisa complains to me about Prince Gunther's immature behavior, I just laugh (to myself. It is rude to mock another person's behavior, no matter how heinous. A true royal is merely inwardly amused by it, according to my grandmother).

I know it's not very royal of me to find the fact

that my cousin and Prince Gunther break up all the time amusing, but I can't help it. Maybe Luisa is right, and I *am* immature.

But I'm definitely *not* a stick-in-the-mud! I like to have fun. I had more fun than anyone over the summer, learning to take my pony, Chrissy, over jumps, playing floating table tennis with my stepbrother, Rocky, or Michael or my dad or my new stepmom, Helen Thermopolis, or even Prince Khalil (the few times he came over before his country imploded), and watching teen movies with my sister, Mia.

I was writing back:

Yes, you are family, Luisa, which means you should be more understanding, and also that you shouldn't call me stupid names such as Stick—

when the voice of Madame Alain herself came on over the school intercom.

"Excuse me, Your Royal Majesties, Highnesses, Graces, lords, ladies, and gentlemen," she said. "I have a special announcement to make. First, I would like to say congratulations to our own Princess Olivia and the rest of the royal family on the historic birth of the new heirs to the throne of Genovia."

Everyone in class turned toward me and began to applaud—which is ridiculous, because *I* hadn't done anything.

But one of the rules of being royal is that you're supposed to accept compliments graciously—Grandmère says it's rude to say "Oh, please, stop," or "Me? No, *you're* the one with the great hair" or whatever.

So I stood up, murmured "Thank you" in the native languages of my various classmates (something else I'd practiced all summer), and sat down again, aware that Prince Khalil was one of the people applauding the loudest and smiling the most at me.

Well, I guess that made sense. I had taken Grandmère's advice (even though Dad had called it melodramatic nonsense) and made a special effort to be kind to him . . . if you could call telling someone in the class cloakroom while hanging up your coat that you're pretty sure you saw a Karpathos frog in the Royal Genovian Gardens the night before being kind.

"A Karpathos frog?" Prince Khalil's dark eyebrows had flown up. "Are you sure? Because those are native to a tiny island in Greece. And they're critically endangered. It would be extremely unlikely to find one here in Genovia."

"Oh, I'm sure," I'd said.

I was sure, too. I *had* seen a frog in the gardens last night.

It just probably wasn't a Karpathos frog.

But it had been worth it to lie, since some of the sadness had left Prince Khalil's eyes. He'd even smiled a little.

Mia says it's all right to lie if the lie makes someone feel better.

Unfortunately our discussion of the Karpathos frog I may or may not have seen in the Royal Genovian Gardens didn't last very long since my cousin Luisa chose that moment to come bursting into the cloakroom, demanding to know if we'd seen a solid-gold Chanel cell phone case she'd dropped earlier that morning. That kind of thing tends to put a damper on any conversation.

Meanwhile, Madame Alain's announcements buzzed on and on.

"Secondly, I regret to inform you that while we did receive enough permission slips this morning to keep from canceling our trip to the Royal School Winter Games this year, we do not have enough chaperones."

There was a gasp from some of the people in class when she said this. Well, from one person, really: Prince Gunther.

"The only way we'll be able to approve this trip is for those of you who've signed up to *please* ask your parents, legal guardians, and other relatives over the age of eighteen to consider chaperoning. I understand that many of them might be suffering from La Grippe at the moment, but if they are healthy enough—and noncontagious—we would certainly appreciate it. All expenses for the trip will, of course, be paid by the Royal Genovian Academy athletic association, and as Stockerdörfl truly is a winter wonderland this time of year, there is no doubt that they will enjoy it."

I heard snickering and turned my head to see where it was coming from. Some of the boys—specifically the 12th Duke of Marborough and the 17th Marquis of Tottingham—were repeating "Stockerdörfl" and "winter wonderland" and laughing.

The words *did* sound kind of funny if you said them out loud.

Prince Gunther, seated a couple of desks away, did not find them that way, however. He'd begun beaming with pride the moment the name of his hometown—Stockerdörfl—was mentioned, but now he was frowning at the snickering boys.

"It's not funny, guys," he whispered. "Stockerdörfl really *is* beautiful this time of year. And you know that the Winter Games are very important. We've got to go. We have to win! We've got to beat TRAIS!"

The boys who'd been laughing at the word "Stockerdörfl" now laughed at Prince Gunther. "Oh, do vee? Do vee *haf* to vin ze Vinter Games?"

Because Prince Gunther is from Austria and English is his second language, he has a bit of an accent. His *w*'s sound like *v*'s and his *v*'s sound like *f*'s. Also, because his parents travel a lot, he's a boarding student at the RGA, and the school has become his second home. He loves it almost as much as he loves his native Stockerdörfl.

But that's no reason to make fun of him.

"How *wery* important are they, Your Highness?" the 12th Duke of Marborough taunted him.

Prince Khalil looked up from the book he was reading on the care and keeping of leopard geckos and said, "Cut it out, Marby."

The Duke of Marborough did cut it out. Because Prince Khalil is the most popular boy in our class, and when he says something, everyone listens and does what he says without even questioning it—even the teachers. He has one of those personalities.

Or it could be the haunting look of loss in his eyes.

"Sorry, Leel," Roger—that's the 12th Duke of Marborough's real name—said, using Prince Khalil's nickname—his name is pronounced *Kuh-LEEL*. Most of the boys call him Leel for short, which I guess is better than Kuh. It is certainly better than Stick.

"Yeah, sorry," Tots, the Marquis of Tottingham, said, and Prince Khalil nodded to him and went back to his book. Even Monsieur Chaudhary, who'd been about to shout at all of them, relaxed back into his seat.

The situation was *handled*.

"If I do not receive the name of at least *one more* volunteer chaperone by six o'clock this evening," Madame Alain continued, "the athletes from this school will not be attending the Winter Games tomorrow for the first time in their one-hundred-and-fifty-year existence, which will be a sad disappointment for *all* of you. And that is because if this school does not have a delegation on the train to Stockerdörfl tomorrow, you will *all* be spending the day writing an eight-hundred-word essay entitled 'The True Meaning of School Spirit, and How I Failed Myself—and My Classmates.'"

There was a good deal of moaning in the language lab at this—but none of it from me.

Because I would much rather write an eight-hundred-word essay on my lack of school spirit than go to some ski resort in the Alps and miss seeing my brand-new niece and nephew come home from the hospital (especially since that's when their heads are going to stop being pointy, and they are going to start being cute, according to my research).

Although now that I think about it, maybe this does sort of make me sound like a stick-in-the-mud.

Could Luisa be right? *Am* I a stick?

Le Palais de Genovia
by the order of
Her Royal Highness Princess
Amelia Mignonette Grimaldi
Thermopolis Renaldo
is pleased to announce the arrival
of
A daughter
5 pounds, 3 ounces
and
A son
5 pounds, 4 ounces
on Tuesday, twenty-fourth November
at
3:22 A.M. and
3:26 A.M GST

Tuesday, November 24
1:00 P.M.
Royal Genovian Academy
Dining Room

Ugh. UGGGGGGH.

Letting us choose our own seats at lunchtime isn't working out *AT ALL*.

Because guess who chose a seat next to me and my best friend (in Genovia), Princess Komiko?

My cousin Lady Luisa Ferrari.

"What's wrong with your sister and Prince Michael?" Luisa wanted to know. She'd read the bulletin that Madame Alain had posted outside the dining room as soon as the Royal Genovian Press Office released it (which of course was right before lunch). "Why won't they tell us the names? Are they having trouble thinking of some? I can give them plenty of ideas. What's wrong with Addison? Or Mason? Those are awesome names."

My other cousin Victorine wrinkled her nose. "I don't think Princess Addison sounds very royal. Or Prince Mason, either."

Silently, I agreed with Victorine, but aloud I said only, "Mia and Michael have plenty of ideas for names. They just want to get to know the babies before making their choices final and announcing them formally."

"I think that's nice," piped up Nadia, one of the new girls who Princess Komiko and I like, and who we always ask to join our table. We've had many new students at the RGA this year, on account of all the refugees from disaster-torn countries seeking asylum in Genovia. "It's wrong to rush into something as important as choosing a name for a baby. It's something he or she is going to be stuck with for his or her whole life."

"Thank you, Nadia," I said. "I think it's important, too."

"Well, so long as they don't choose something boring." Luisa still looked unimpressed. "Have you heard what the bookies in Las Vegas are saying the names are going to be?" When we all stared at her blankly, she went on, "Elizabeth! Can you believe it? And Frank. Don't even ask me why. I mean, Elizabeth is all right, I guess. Who ever heard of a prince named *Frank*?"

I sat there in complete shock, unable to say a word for a moment.

Of course it was possible the bookies were wrong—they'd been wrong about both the babies being girls, and look at the mess they'd gotten me into with Nishi!

But what if they were right about this one? Could Mia and Michael really be naming their daughter Elizabeth—which was the name of my dead mother? (I barely remember her. She was a charter jet pilot who'd died when I was a baby in a tragic personal watercraft accident.)

But if they'd chosen the name Frank for their little boy, it seemed possible.

"Frank was the name of Princess Mia's stepdad, who was Rocky's father," I heard myself murmuring. "Frank Gianini. He died a few years ago."

"Awwww." Victorine laid a hand over her heart, as if she was so touched, she'd burst a heartstring. "That is so sad! But it's so *cute* that they're naming the baby after him!" All the other girls at nearby tables—even some seniors!—overheard, and did the same thing with their hands, nodding in agreement. "What a touching tribute."

"But we don't even know for sure that those are the names they've chosen," I said quickly. "How could those people in Las Vegas know when they haven't mentioned anything to *me* about it?"

"Thank goodness!" Luisa cried. "Because Prince Frank is just an *awful* name."

That's when Prince Gunther, coming to my sister's defense, said, "Frank is a very old and noble name in my culture, Luisa. It means a free man . . . or a type of javelin."

Everyone looked at him strangely. *Javelin?*

Prince Gunther is much less weird than he used to be, thanks to Lady Luisa Ferrari. In between their fights, she has been slowly socializing him. Gone are his athletic socks, shower sandals, and chlorine-green blond hair. Luisa even bought them matching silver bracelets that say *L + G*!

But he still comes out with an occasional odd statement.

Not as weird, however, as the things his girl-friend sometimes says, such as what she said to me next, which was:

"This must be a really sad day for you, Princess Olivia."

"Sad?" I stared at her. "Why on earth should I be sad?"

"Because until today, you were next in line to the throne after your sister. Now you're *third*, after the babies. You're what they call the 'spare heir.'"

The chicken piccata I'd been chewing nearly dropped out of my mouth, I was so shocked. "You think I'd rather have a stupid throne than a new *niece and nephew*?"

"Who wouldn't?" Luisa asked with a shrug. "I'd much rather rule a country than have a couple of dribbling babies living in my palace." She turned toward Prince Gunther. "Wouldn't you?"

Prince Gunther looked uncomfortable. "Er, well . . . I don't—"

"Luisa," I said, annoyed, "I know you don't have any sisters or brothers, so you don't know what it's like to be an aunt. But trust me, it's much better than being the heir to a throne."

"Yeah, Luisa," Victorine said. "Even though Olivia isn't as close to inheriting the throne as she was, she still gets all the benefits of being a princess. She gets to live in a palace—"

"The *summer palace*," Luisa pointed out. "Isn't your dad renovating the *summer palace* for you and your stepmother and Rocky to live in?"

I shrugged. "Yeah? So what?" The renovation was taking forever, since the ancient foundation was crumbling, and the whole place had to be shored up to keep it from sinking back into the Genovian earth. My dad spends all day on the phone, yelling at contractors to find out why it isn't done.

"It's still a *palace*," Victorine snapped. "And Princess Olivia gets amazing designer clothes to wear, her own hair and wardrobe stylists, and her own limousines and bodyguards."

"And a pony," Princess Komiko added. "Don't forget the pony."

Nadia sighed. "I don't even know what I'm going to get you for your birthday. You have every-thing!"

"Don't get me anything!" I cried, mortified. "Like it said on the invitation, the gift of your presence at my party is present enough."

"Could we get back to the topic at hand?" Luisa demanded, clearly annoyed.

"You mean how we're all going to have to write an eight-hundred-word essay tomorrow and miss going to the most beautiful place on earth if we don't find a chaperone for the school trip?" Prince Gunther asked. "Yes, I would very much like to talk about this."

"No," Luisa said, rolling her eyes. "How Olivia still has to put up with all the worst parts of being a princess, like having paparazzi take unflattering photos of her every time she's in a swimsuit, and having to do all that gross charity stuff, like visiting people in the hospital who have La Grippe, but she's never going to get to rule."

This has actually never happened—but only because no one with La Grippe has ever been sick enough to be hospitalized.

"So what, Luisa?" I said, feeling as annoyed with her as she clearly was with me. "My sister's babies are really cute. Here, take a look."

Even though we're not supposed to use our cell phones during school hours, I thought showing Luisa the photos I'd snapped of the twins might convince her of how dumb she was being.

Big mistake.

"Um," Luisa said, squinting down at my cell phone's screen. "What's wrong with their heads?"

"Nothing," I said defensively—although of course I knew exactly what she was talking about. "Why?"

Nadia peeked over Luisa's arm so that she could see the photos, too.

"They're newborns," Nadia said. "That's how newborns are supposed to look."

"Excuse me," Luisa said. "But who asked you?"

Luisa Ferrari is never nice to anyone, but she's particularly mean to the refugees, despite Madame Alain urging us to be friendly to them, since they've lost almost everything they had, including their homes, possessions, and in some cases, even family members. It's our duty as royals—and fellow human beings on this planet—to show them kindness and generosity, just like Grandmère said I was to do for Prince Khalil now that he'd lost his kingdom.

But this is difficult for Luisa.

"Also, you're wrong, Nadia," Luisa said. "I've seen newborn babies before, and they don't look like that."

"Where have you seen newborns?" I asked.

"On TV," Luisa said firmly. "I've seen every single episode of *Law and Order: SVU*, and none of the newborn babies abandoned in Dumpsters on that show look like little frogs, like those two."

I felt my temper rise even further. Frogs? My niece and nephew do *not* look like frogs. I'd just seen a frog, so I could attest to this.

Luisa was about to get a piece of my mind when Nadia came to the rescue.

"They're not allowed to use real newborns on TV." Nadia had been a tween star on a soap opera in her home country before its film industry had been shut down by the war there, so she would know. "It's against the law. Babies have to be two weeks old before they can appear on film."

"Well, even so, there must be something wrong with Princess Mia's new babies," Luisa said with a sniff. "Because they look terrible."

"There's nothing wrong with them," I snapped. "The doctor said they're fine. They're full term and everything. But you know, human babies and kangaroo babies have a lot in common."

"Kangaroo babies?"

"Yes," I said. I don't know why. I should have taken Luisa's expression as my cue to shut up, but I didn't. "Most mammals are born with the ability to walk and feed themselves, but both human babies and kangaroos are born completely dependent on their mothers. Kangaroo babies are only about an inch long when they're born, and they have to crawl all the way up from the birth canal into their mother's pouch in order to continue to grow into the cute roos we all remember from *Winnie-the-Pooh*. But unlike frogs, they're still *mammals*, at least."

I could tell from the look on Luisa's face that I'd gone too far. This happens sometimes. As a future wildlife illustrator, I'm slightly obsessed with animals. I've been warned—especially by Nishi—that occasionally I talk about them in a little too much detail.

Luisa dropped her fork. "Birth canal? Excuse me while I vomit, please. How are we supposed to eat with *that* image in our heads?"

Uh-oh. I'd done it again.

"I think it's pretty interesting," chimed a new voice.

Luisa whirled around so quickly that her long hair flew out and hit me—and Princess Komiko—in the face. "Oh! Prince Khalil! I didn't notice you standing there."

Neither had I.

But it turned out Prince Khalil had been standing quite nearby, holding a plate of cheesecake from the dessert trolley. Normally a dining staff member pushes the dessert trolley from table to table, asking students what they'd like. But with so many people taken ill with La Grippe lately, they'd had to make dessert self-serve.

"Thanks," I said to Prince Khalil, hoping he wouldn't notice my blushing cheeks. (Contrary to Luisa's often-voiced opinion, black people do blush. I even got sunburned a few times while playing floating table tennis for too long without reapplying my sunscreen.) "Kangaroos *are* extremely interesting."

I was trying to think of something witty to say about the birth habits of kangaroos, when, to my absolute astonishment, Prince Khalil sat down in one of the empty chairs at our table.

It wasn't exactly strange for him to do this. We used to be friends.

I simply wasn't expecting it after what had happened yesterday, with the whole *You're the opposite of a dork* incident.

Maybe my being kind to him in the cloakroom (and lying about having seen a Karpathos frog in the Royal Genovian Gardens) had worked!

This probably would have been a good opportunity to take one (or more) of the photos I owed Nishi. She'd already texted me several times this morning to remind me about them:

> Congratulations! You're an aunt. And I was right ☺ ☺ ☺!!! It's a boy AND a girl! I can't wait to get my photos of Prince Khalil. Please take and send ASAP. If you can get one of him shirtless at the beach, that would be great. Luv u!!!!!

But nowhere had we specified in our deal that I had to send the photos *the same day* the twins were born.

And besides, it would look weird if I started taking photos of Prince Khalil in the dining hall while he was sitting next to me eating cheesecake . . .

. . . which reminds me, I better stop writing in here while he's talking to me, or it will look like I'm not paying attention. One of the main rules of being a royal *and* a good friend is that it's important to look like you're paying attention when ~~the boy you like is sitting right next to you eating cheesecake~~ someone is talking to you, especially someone who has lost their kingdom to their despotic uncle.

Tuesday, November 24
3:15 P.M.
Royal Limousine

Well, that was a disaster.

This whole day has been a disaster, really.

Not that becoming an aunt isn't *amazing*.

But everything else about this day? Not so good.

The worst part was when Prince Khalil asked, as he was eating his cheesecake (not while his mouth was full, since that would have been gross, and he is very polite), "So, Princess Olivia, have you changed your mind about attending the Royal School Winter Games?"

I thought Luisa—who overheard this—was going to choke on her vichyssoise.

"*Her?*" she exclaimed. "*She's* not going."

Prince Khalil looked concerned. "Really? Still? Why not?"

"Oh, well," I said, trying to appear casual. "Because I became an aunt today, you know—OW."

The *OW* was because someone at the table suddenly kicked my ankle—hard—underneath the tablecloth. I looked accusingly at Luisa. The kick had come from her direction.

"Is something wrong?" Prince Khalil asked, looking even more concerned. Nishi is right about his eyebrows, I've noticed. It's nice when they get that squinchy look in the middle when he's being very serious about something.

"Oh, no," I said, reaching down to rub my ankle. Luisa always wears super high heels with pointy toes. "Everything is fine. The truth is, I'm—OW!"

Luisa kicked me again, this time getting my fingers.

"What's wrong with you?" I hissed at her.

"What's wrong with *me*?" she hissed back. "What's wrong with *you* . . . *Stick*?"

I scowled at her. "Don't call me that."

"Why not? You *are* one."

"I am not."

Prince Khalil glanced from one of us to the other in confusion. "I'm sorry," he said. "Am I interrupting something?"

"No," I said quickly.

"Yes," Luisa said. "But only the fact that my cousin Princess Olivia would rather write an eight-hundred-word essay and hang around with some dribbling little babies than go skiing in the Alps with all of her classmates."

"Luisa," I hissed, "I don't even know how to ski. Remember?"

Luisa's big blue eyes widened. "Oh, that's right! I forgot!" Then she burst out laughing. Hard. "Ha ha ha! Stick can't ski!"

Seriously? I wanted to say to her. Not everyone grew up in a CASTLE, with rich parents who bought them everything they wanted and took them on fancy ski vacations (until they got divorced) like you, Luisa.

And okay, technically Luisa didn't grow up in a castle. It was a villa.

But the rest of that statement is true.

My aunt and uncle in New Jersey—with whom I lived before finding out I was a princess and moving to Genovia—had never taken me on vacation, let alone a *ski* vacation.

So I have no idea how to ski, snowboard, skate, or even sled, except for the sledding Nishi and I had done in Nishi's backyard, which hardly counts.

So even if I'd wanted to go—which I hadn't—there'd never seemed like much point in me attending the Royal School Winter Games. I had refrained from mentioning it at home, and conveniently "lost" all permission slips pertaining to it. I knew there wasn't anything to worry about where Rocky was concerned: He immediately forgets everything to do with school the moment he gets home to the palace.

"Wait." Prince Gunther, who had overheard, looked as if someone had just switched a light on inside his head. "That's right! I forgot you've never skied before, Princess Olivia. But that's okay. I can teach you!"

"Uh . . ." I said. "Thank you, Prince Gunther. But that's really not—"

"No," Prince Gunther cried. "I am the best ski instructor in all of Stockerdörfl! Everyone says so. Come on the trip, and I can teach you to ski!"

"She isn't going to be able to learn in time to compete," Luisa said, not laughing anymore. In fact, she looked a bit angry. "That's if we even still go to Stockerdörfl, which is getting more and more doubtful considering we don't have enough chaperones . . . remember? And Olivia doesn't even *want* to go. She said herself she'd rather stay home with her new little baby niece and—"

"But you *must* go, Princess Olivia," Prince Gunther said, turning his bright-eyed gaze toward me. "Even if you don't compete, the school could still use your help! Your cousin Marguerite is out sick with La Grippe, isn't she?"

"It's true," said Victorine. "Poor Marguerite

hasn't been to school since last week, she's had such a bad cough, runny nose, and sore throat. She says her mom is driving her *crazy*. She won't even let her watch movies because she says the glare from the screen might give her a migraine."

Prince Gunther continued, as if Victorine hadn't interrupted, "Marguerite was supposed to photograph us for the school yearbook and newspaper—"

"Yep," Victorine said. "Marguerite is in charge of photography. I'm in charge of layout because I'm so fashion conscious." Victorine pointed to her combat boots. "As you can probably tell."

"You are obviously very skilled with a camera, Princess Olivia," Prince Gunther went on, "because you took those very cute photos of your sweet little niece and nephew."

"Ew," Luisa said. "You actually thought those photos she took were good?"

"I thought they were," Prince Khalil said. I'd shown them to him when he'd asked what everyone was talking about.

"Thanks," I said, and smiled at him.

He actually smiled back. "You're welcome."

It was working! My campaign to be kind to him was working!

What was it about Prince Khalil's smile—and his darkly lashed eyes—that gave me such a weird feeling inside, almost like I'd just raced Rocky up the Grand Royal Staircase?

I don't know, but I had to admit, I kind of liked it.

"And you will love Stockerdörfl," Prince Gunther gushed. "It is not warm like Genovia this time of year, but the snow is deep and beautiful, and everyone sits by the warm fire feeling so jolly, drinking hot apple cider, and singing our native songs."

"Yeah, Olivia," Luisa said, smirking at me. "Don't you want to sit around the warm fire, drinking hot apple cider and feeling so jolly? What is wrong with you?"

"Nothing," I said. "I just—"

"I'm going," Prince Khalil said. "I'm competing on the RGA hockey team."

This caused my eyes to widen. "YOU play hockey?"

"Yes," he said. "Hockey is my favorite sport."

I guess I could see how Prince Khalil, who was so fond of reptiles, would like hockey as well. Both hockey and catching iguanas require cages and having good aim.

"I'm going, too," Nadia chimed in. "I'm competing in the singles figure skating."

Luisa gave her the evil eye. "So am I. I didn't even know they *had* ice-skating rinks in your country."

"Of course we do." Nadia evil-eyed her right back. "At least, we did."

Princess Komiko said, to no one in particular, "I'm competing in the ski jumping."

Victorine looked at her in surprise. "You *are*?"

"Yes," Princess Komiko said. "Why?"

"No reason," Victorine said, but I knew the reason why: Princess Komiko is so shy, it's hard to imagine her doing something as daring as flying down a hill on a pair of skis, then jumping off it.

But if there's one thing I've learned, it's that everyone has hidden strengths (and weaknesses).

It's finding out these things about the people you know that makes life so interesting.

"So perhaps if you won't compete, you would take over as official school photographer?" Prince Gunther asked me, ignoring the other girls. "Also, my parents will be hosting a very nice dinner in my home on Thursday night for all the students and parents from the RGA. It would be such an honor if you were there. Please say you will come."

Well, this was awkward. How could I say no when Prince Gunther was being so nice?

"It's so sweet of you to ask," I said. "But my family really needs me at home."

Fortunately Luisa was there—as always—to help me out (not).

"Now you're just being selfish, Olivia. If you don't come, we won't have enough chaperones, and Madame Alain is going to cancel the whole trip, and we're all going to have to stay here and write essays."

"How will that be my fault?" I demanded. "I don't come with a chaperone."

"Yes, you do," Victorine pointed out. "Everywhere you go, you bring a bodyguard."

"Princess Olivia's bodyguard will be busy bodyguarding *her*," Prince Khalil said. "She won't have time to chaperone anyone else."

I was so relieved that he'd pointed this out—so I didn't have to—I wanted to hug him, or at least thank him very politely.

"Why don't you ask your stepmother, Olivia?" Victorine cried. "Helen Thermopolis is so cool!"

Princess Komiko gasped. "Yes! Princess Helen! Ask her, Olivia, please."

My stepmother, Helen Thermopolis—or *Princess* Helen Thermopolis as she is officially known now that she and my dad had gotten quietly married over the summer—had visited the RGA several times to speak about contemporary women artists, since she is one.

During her talks at school, Helen had discussed the things she feels passionately about, including:

- Art
- Gender equality
- Following one's dreams, and
- The importance of parents not overscheduling children, and also giving them ample time away from screens. Helen believes the only way people (both young and old) can discover what they're truly good at is if they have time to be bored.

"When we are bored," Helen said, "we naturally gravitate toward the things that interest us the most. These are generally the things at which we turn out to be the most talented, whether it's cooking, gardening, gymnastics, computer engineering, physics, auto mechanics, woodworking, parkour, or whatever."

In Helen's case, it was painting. In my sister's case, it was writing and political activism. In Prince Khalil's case, it was herpetology (and apparently hockey). In Rocky's case, it's been inventing things, such as rocket ships. In mine, it's wildlife illustration, horseback riding, and floating table tennis.

"Well," I said hesitantly. "I *guess* I could ask her . . ."

"Great!" Victorine said. "It's all settled then! Olivia is going to ask her stepmom to be our chaperone, then come with us to Stockerdörfl. This is going to be *fantastic*!"

Victorine, Prince Gunther, Nadia, Princess Komiko, and even a grudgingly accepting Luisa all fist-bumped one another (Luisa probably because Helen also believes in letting kids do pretty much whatever they want, so long as it's not dangerous or illegal).

Only Prince Khalil seemed to sense that I wasn't quite as enthusiastic as everyone else seemed.

"I'm sorry," he leaned over to say in a low voice, so the others wouldn't hear. "I know you said yesterday that you didn't want to go to Stockerdörfl. I didn't mean to make things more complicated for you."

He looked worried . . . worried for me!

I couldn't believe it. I'm not the one whose country has been taken over by a despotic megalomaniac.

"No," I said. "It's okay. I'll figure it out."

I didn't want to burden him with my problems, considering the fact that his problems are so much more serious than mine. Instead I tried to smile bravely, because that's what princesses are supposed to do. My royal relatives have had to deal with much worse stuff than cousins who keep insisting they are immature sticks-in-the-mud. There's a painting in the hall of portraits of one of my ancestresses, Princess Mathilde the Brave, who once drove invading marauders away from the palace by ordering that boiling oil be poured down on them from the parapets.

My problems (such as not being able to ski, or having to ask my stepmother to chaperone a school trip the same week her daughter's twins were born) seem quite silly compared to that.

But evidently my smile wasn't brave enough to convince Prince Khalil, since he asked, still looking concerned, "Would you like me to get you some cheesecake? The bell hasn't rung yet." He smiled—not bravely, but very, very kindly. "And cheesecake generally makes everything better."

For some reason, his concern—or maybe his

smile—made my pulse speed up a little. Had I ever told him that the Cheesecake Factory used to be my favorite restaurant (until I moved to Genovia, where there are even better restaurants than the Cheesecake Factory)? How had he known how much I love cheesecake? Or does everyone love cheesecake?

(Actually this isn't true. Nishi hates cheesecake. Should I tell Nishi that Prince Khalil likes cheesecake and that maybe because of this, the two of them wouldn't make that good of a couple? Or would that be mean of me?)

And how nice of him to offer to get me some! I had never seen Prince Gunther offer to get Luisa cheesecake. . . .

But then again, I'd never seen Luisa eat cheesecake, as she is always on a diet.

"Um," I said, "yes. I would love some cheesecake. But I can get it myself—"

But before I could assure Prince Khalil that I was perfectly capable of getting my own cheesecake from the dessert cart (which is something Helen Thermopolis *and* my sister would have wanted me to do), he was already up and getting it for me, and Luisa was staring daggers at me from across the table.

What? I mouthed at her. After all, it wasn't *my* fault Prince Khalil wanted to get me cheesecake. Luisa's boyfriend was perfectly capable of getting her cheesecake if he wanted to.

Not that Prince Khalil is my boyfriend.

Luisa said, "Nice going, Stick." But she didn't say it in a mean way. There was a tiny smile on her lip-glossed face.

I don't know what she meant by that.

And it didn't matter, anyway, because just then the bells started to ring. Not only the bell to signify that lunch was over, but all the bells in the entire city, to celebrate the births of my new niece and nephew.

So I never ended up getting my cheesecake from Prince Khalil anyway.

Tuesday, November 24
5:15 P.M.
Royal Genovian Gardens

When I got home I found Rocky outside by the pool. He gets out of school a half hour earlier than I do because he's in the lower form, and Genovians believe younger children need less time in school than older children.

(Which makes no sense. Younger children have more to learn than older children, but whatever.)

He was sitting on one of the silver serving trays from the sets they use for high tea. He'd poured crushed ice from the kitchens all over the grass, put

the tray on the ice, and was holding the end of Snowball's leash while yelling "Mush!" at her.

But Snowball was only sitting there in front of him and the tray, not moving, wagging her tail and yawning in the hot afternoon sun.

"What are you doing?" I demanded.

"I'm trying to train your dog to be a sled dog," Rocky replied. "But as you can see, she's useless."

"Snowball is not useless," I informed him, snatching the leash from him. "She's just not a sled dog. She is not a service dog of any kind. Snowball, are you all right?"

Snowball jumped around and licked me in the face while I inspected her for injuries.

"She's fine," Rocky said. "She liked it. And poodles are too service dogs. In olden times they used to help during hunts and stuff. They dove into the water and fetched dead ducks."

"Well, that isn't quite the same as pulling sleds, is it?"

"I guess not. But I need to enter into some kind of sport at the Royal School Winter Games if I'm going to get out of school this week," Rocky said. "I don't want to sit around and write some dumb essay. And sled dog racing seems like the most exciting."

"Well, you're not using MY dog for it." I hugged Snowball, who continued to wag her tail and lick me, seemingly unharmed. "She's never even seen snow! How is she going to know how to pull a sled?"

"That," Rocky said tiredly, "is what I was trying to teach her when you came along—"

"Shhh!" Grandmère rose up from one of the chaise longues, where she'd apparently been sitting in a caftan and a large sun hat, enjoying a cocktail. "What are you two fussing about? Don't you know there are babies in the palace?"

"Oh, sorry, Grandmère," I said, instantly feeling guilty. "We were just, uh—"

"I need a sport if I'm going to the Royal School Winter Games tomorrow," Rocky announced, in what was, for him, a whisper, but for anyone else would have been a normal speaking voice. "Olivia won't let me use Snowball as a sled dog. Can I borrow Rommel?"

"Not only CAN you not, you MAY not," Grandmère said. "Rommel was not bred to pull sleds. He is a companion animal of much empathy and refinement."

I didn't want to point out to Grandmère that even as she said this, Rommel was sitting behind her in the grass, licking his own butt.

"And what do you mean, the Royal School Winter Games are tomorrow?" Grandmère asked. "They can't possibly be. They don't hold the Royal School Winter Games until November—" Her voice trailed off and she got a faraway look in her eye. "Good heavens."

"Yes," I said. "But don't worry, Grandmère. The Royal Genovian Academy isn't going."

"What?" Grandmère and Rocky both cried at the same time.

"They're not," I said. "Because of La Grippe, we don't have enough chaperones. So Madame Alain is canceling our participation in the Games."

"That is an outrage!" cried Grandmère, gesturing so dramatically that she spilled half her cocktail. Snowball and Rommel hurried to lick it up, but it got absorbed too quickly into the hot terrazzo. "The Royal Genovian Academy *always* participates in the Winter Games!"

"Well," I said, "I suppose so, but Rocky and I couldn't go anyway. We have the babies to think of."

"The babies?" Grandmère sipped what was left of her cocktail. "The *babies*? The babies will be able to get along quite well without you. The babies won't even be able to recognize you for months—years if they've inherited their grandfather's vision. But what possible point is there in holding the Royal School Winter Games without a representative of the Royal

House of Renaldo present, much less the Royal Genovian Academy? Why, this is an outrage! Do you know that I won the cross-country ski competition every year I attended?"

I was surprised. "No, Grandmère, I didn't."

"Yes! Eight years in a row! Not only did I win, but I broke what was then a local record—in the women's biathlon, no less."

I realized maybe I shouldn't have been surprised. "Grandmère, doesn't the biathlon involve skiing cross country and then shooting rifles at a target?"

"It most certainly does."

This explained a lot. Grandmère loves shooting at things, most particularly the iguanas that took over her beloved rose garden last spring. This was why Prince Khalil had had to come over and remove them—the iguanas, not the roses—in a safe and humane manner. Fortunately (or not so fortunately, for the footmen) Grandmère's aim had gotten pretty bad over the years.

"I have never heard of anything as preposterous as not attending the Games. And for such an absurd reason . . . not enough chaperones—and all because they are suffering from something as trifling as a little cold. Why, we attended the Games *during the war*!"

Whenever Grandmère mentions "the war," she means World War II, when Nazis invaded Genovia and took over not only its government and seaport (advantageously tucked between France and Italy) but its lucrative fruit and olive oil industry, and even the palace.

"Not, of course, that we allowed this to bother us," Grandmère went on. "Genovia was the jewel in the crown of the Führer's empire, but we carried on working against him beneath his very nose. When the Royal School Winter Games came along, we used them as an opportunity to deliver messages over the Austrian border to the Allies. We beat them. By sheer determination alone—yes, we beat them all, by God!"

"Did you shoot any Nazis?" Rocky asked, looking excited.

"Did I shoot any Nazis," Grandmère murmured.

"I did far worse to them than shoot them, young man."

Rocky began to jump up and down excitedly. "Like what? Tell me, tell me!"

Above us, a pair of French doors opened, and a second later, Mia stepped out onto one of the balconies overlooking the palace pool.

"Excuse me," she said politely. "But could the three of you possibly take your conversation— whatever it's about—somewhere else?"

Rocky shaded his eyes with his hand and blinked up at Mia. "But Mia, Grandmère was about to tell us about the Nazis!"

Mia did not look very approving. "Oh, was she? Well, Michael and I finally got both babies to sleep at the same time, and now we'd like to try to get some sleep ourselves, so perhaps you'd like to talk about the Nazis somewhere else? The billiard room, perhaps? Or the library?"

I gasped. "Oh, Mia! I'm sorry we were being too loud."

"I'm sorry, too," Rocky said. "Those little babies

really need their sleep if their heads are ever going to look normal."

"What?" Mia asked, looking confused.

"Nothing," Grandmère said, taking Rocky by the shoulder and steering him away from the balcony. "Never mind. The babies are beautiful. So sorry to have woken them, Amelia. Get back to your nap."

Mia smiled, then thanked us and went back inside. Rocky immediately tugged on the draping sleeve of Grandmère's caftan. "You're going to tell us more about the Nazis, aren't you, Grandmère?"

"I'll do better than that," Grandmère said. "I'll call your school right now and personally give them a piece of my mind. I never heard of anything more disgraceful than Genovia not taking part in the Royal School Winter Games!"

So . . . great.

I'm the only one who *doesn't* want to go to Stockerdörfl tomorrow, but my grandmother is the person fighting hardest to make sure my school goes.

Fantastic.

Tuesday, November 24
8:30 P.M.
Royal Genovian Bedroom

The worst thing ever has just happened. I mean literally the WORST.

We were having a "light supper" because Chef Bernard has come down with La Grippe—so instead of the usual six courses, we were only having five: an appetizer, entrée, salad, cheese course, then dessert . . . no soup, which of course made Grandmère complain like crazy. "What is a meal," she kept asking, "without soup?"—when the royal obstetrician asked for an audience.

This made me almost drop my fork. I was sure there had to be an emergency with Mia or the babies.

And it turned out there was. Just not one where anyone was dramatically carried off in an ambulance.

Dr. Khan, the royal obstetrician, came in and curtsied and said how sorry she was to interrupt our dinner, but that she had something of vital importance she needed to discuss . . . and the something turned out to be ME AND ROCKY!

"Your Highness," she said to Dad, as he sat there with a wineglass in his hand (he'd offered some Genovian pinot noir to the obstetrician, but she said she still had rounds to make), "I feel I must tell you that it is in the best interest of your two new grandchildren to keep them as far as possible from all potential carriers of influenza A."

Dad looked startled. "What? Of course! Wait . . . what is influenza A?"

"La Grippe," said Dr. Khan.

"Good lord," cried Grandmère, dropping her cheeseknife. "The babies have La Grippe?"

"Not at all," said Dr. Khan. "But I understand that your chef has been exposed to it, and I've just been speaking to Princess Mia, who says a number of students and faculty at the Royal Genovian Academy have it. I would like to suggest limiting your children's exposure to Princess Mia and the babies for the next few days."

Dad looked from the doctor to Rocky and me. "You want me to put my own children out of the house?"

"I would not suggest it to just anyone, Your Highness," the doctor said, smiling a little. "But I do believe you have the resources to find alternative accommodations for them. I think it would be the sensible thing to do. The virus is quite dangerous to infants, and Princess Mia would rest easier."

"Pfuit!" Grandmère made her traditional noise of contempt and rolled her eyes at me. "Your sister has always been such a hypochondriac."

But I didn't think Mia was being a hypochondriac. If I had newborn twins, I wouldn't want them being exposed to La Grippe, either.

"Maybe," I said, "you should cancel school, Dad."

Rocky gasped. "Yeah!"

This really would be great. Then none of us would have to go to Stockerdörfl—or stay in class and write an eight-hundred-word essay, either.

"I wouldn't go that far," Dr. Khan said. "We haven't quite reached national health emergency proportions. Just a few sensible precautions should take care of the problem—like keeping potential carriers of the virus away from newborns until the babies can build up their immune systems and the carriers can show that they're symptom-free."

Rocky began to cough. "I think I've got it, Dad. I think I've got La Grippe! I think you better send me to Stockerdörfl."

I glared at him from across the table and mouthed the word *faker*. Rocky only smiled at me and fake-coughed some more.

Fortunately, Rocky's mother knew he was faking, too.

"Stop it, Rock," Helen Thermopolis said, then turned to take Dad's hand. "It sounds like a good idea to me, Phillipe. I know it would make Mia feel better."

That's when I knew Rocky and I were in trouble. My heart began to beat a little fast.

Were they seriously suggesting we leave Genovia?

I know I had only lived there a few months, but in that time it had become home—the only place I'd ever really considered home in my life! And now they were going to make me leave it? (Only for a few days, I realized . . . but the thought was terrifying.)

"Do you really want to risk us spreading La Grippe to a foreign land?" I cried, realizing I probably sounded crazy, but not caring. "That sounds pretty undiplomatic to me! It could start a war."

"Well, now," Dad said, signaling the butler to refill his wineglass. "I kind of like the idea of getting you kids out of here for a few days—especially if this virus is as bad as people are saying it is. I don't want either of you to catch it. What do you think, Mother?"

"I think it's the best idea I've heard in ages," Grandmère said, imperiously tapping her own wineglass so the butler would know she, too, would like a refill. "Especially if I go with the children. They need more chaperones for the trip, you know, Phillipe, so I already contacted the school and volunteered my services."

I nearly choked on the sip of water I'd taken. "You *did*?"

"I most certainly did," Grandmère said. "I considered it my duty as a Genovian citizen. Of course Madame Alain was elated and accepted my offer."

"Well," Dad said, turning back toward Dr. Khan. "Then it's all settled. The children—and my mother—are going to Stockerdörfl."

NOOOOOOOOOOOOOOOOOOOOOOOOOOO OOOOOOOOOO!!!!

Tuesday, November 24
9:35 P.M.
Royal Genovian Bedroom

< NishiGirl   **OlivGrace >**

Hi, Olivia, are you there?

Yes, I'm here. How is it going?

Good. So?

So, things are okay. How are things with you?

Things with me are good. You?

< NishiGirl · OlivGrace >

Well, I mean, the royal obstetrician came and said that Dad has to send me and Rocky away for the next few days because we might by carrying the germs of a deadly virus, so I'm being forced to go on a school trip that I don't want to go on that my grandmother is chaperoning. And when my cousin Luisa finds out, she's probably going to kill me, because you know how strict my grandmother is. Luisa isn't going to like it one bit. But I guess other than that things are okay. You?

OMG I meant SO WHERE ARE MY PHOTOS OF PRINCE KHALIL????

Oh, sorry, I haven't gotten them yet. Besides, I thought you liked that boy Dylan from your English class.

I do, but he's no PRINCE. And anyway, I don't have to like just one person. I told you, we're only in 7th grade, we're not getting MARRIED or anything just yet.

HA. But did you know Prince Khalil likes cheesecake?

What does that have to do with anything?

< NishiGirl   OlivGrace >

Well, just that maybe you two wouldn't make the greatest couple. You don't have that much in common.

Like I said, I don't want to marry him, I just want the 4 photos of him that you owe me.

Fine. I'll get them for you. Just give me a little time, would you? There is a lot going on. My sister just had twins, the whole palace is in an uproar over this virus thing, and tomorrow I've got to leave on a ski trip to the Alps, even though I don't even know how to ski.

Oh you poor little baby! Don't forget your pony and cute puppy and the birthday ball in your honor this coming weekend, too. I'm crying for you.

You don't have to be sarcastic about it.

I'm not! I'm merely stating a fact. I wish I were going on a school ski trip to the Alps with a bunch of cute princes.

With your snobby cousin who hates you?

< NishiGirl   OlivGrace >

Ew. Um, OK, maybe not. Is Prince Khalil going on this school ski trip?

That is not the point.

It is if it means you can get me my photos!

Ugh. Uuuuuuuuggggggghhhhhh!

I get what Nishi is saying. From the outside, my life must look pretty great. I know I should be concentrating on all the great things going on, not just in my life but in the world. This is the first time in Genovian history that a firstborn girl will have been given precedence over a younger brother in inheriting the throne! That is all they're talking about on the news (besides La Grippe).

And of course I'm *thrilled* that my sister has given birth to two healthy babies, and that she herself is doing well, especially after all that worry about her blood pressure.

But how am I supposed to get those photos of

Prince Khalil that Nishi wants without looking like a total fool????

You can't go up to a boy and say, "Excuse me, but can I take a few pictures of you for my friend? Okay, great. So just take off your shirt and go stand in front of that sunset and smile. Thanks!"

Well, I suppose *some* girls could do that, but not me.

And especially not a boy like Prince Khalil, who has endured so much heartache, what with losing his country and then deciding not to talk to me ever again (at least, not the way we used to talk).

Not that if things had gone the way I would have wanted them to go—maybe, once upon a time—my dad would have even *let* me go out with Prince Khalil. Once over the summer, when Mia and I were watching one of those teen movies she loves so much, Dad walked in, took one look at the screen, and said that over his dead body would I ever be going out with a boy in middle school. He says it's "inappropriate" for middle schoolers to date, and also ridiculous.

I asked him how old *is* appropriate for girls and boys to date, and he said, "College."

Mia laughed and said, "Dad, stop teasing her."

But I'm pretty sure Dad wasn't teasing.

I think Dad's worried because my sister went on her first date with Michael when she was fourteen—one year older than I am (or than I will be on Saturday)—and look what happened: She ended up marrying him!

Although Mia always points out that she and Michael both dated other people in between their first date and getting married, twelve years later. She says that the road to true love is filled with many unexpected twists, turns, and phonies who only want to marry you for your crown (Grandmère agrees with this).

But the truth is, I don't actually want to date—much less marry—*anyone*. I just want someone to dance with at the ball on Saturday . . . someone who is *not* my dad.

Or Prince Gunther, who always steps on my toes, and is my cousin Luisa's boyfriend.

Wednesday, November 25
8:10 A.M.
Royal Limousine to the Train Station

Francesca is so excited that I'm going somewhere with cold weather, she could hardly contain herself while packing.

"You can finally wear those boots we bought for you in Paris, Your Highness!" she cried. "And that adorable faux-fur zip-up vest!"

I've actually been to cold-weather places since finding out I'm a princess. My dad, Helen, Rocky, and I took a fishing trip to Iceland over the summer for Dad and Helen's honeymoon. I've just never been skiing.

Francesca somehow managed to cram everything Snowball and I needed (because of course I'm bringing Snowball with me. I don't trust anyone to take proper care of her while I'm gone—not with two newborn babies in the palace!) into only two suitcases, which I thought was pretty good . . . especially when the footmen came downstairs with Grandmère's luggage. She had *seventeen* individual valises.

"Mother," Dad said, looking down at Grandmère's pile of Louis Vuitton suitcases. "You're only going away for a couple of days. What on earth are you taking with you—your silver high tea set?"

"You know I must have *my things* about me, Phillipe," Grandmère said, tugging on her mink-lined gloves. "I can't stand to be without *my things*. Now, Amelia, are you certain you can do without us, especially at such a trying time?"

Mia was standing high above us at the top of the Grand Royal Staircase with her daughter in her arms. Michael was holding his son. Both babies were being quiet for once, but this was quite unusual. In the past twenty-four hours or so since they'd come home, unless they were sleeping or eating, one of them was always crying, which usually started the other one crying, and then they'd both be crying.

It didn't matter where you went in the palace—which I used to think was quite large—you could still hear them, even if you put in the earplugs the Royal Genovian Guard use for target practice.

There isn't anything wrong with them, either. They are both perfectly healthy.

It is the worst.

"It will be hard," Michael said to Grandmère. "But we'll try to get on without you, Clarisse . . . at least until the christening, and the bris, of course. But that won't be until next week."

"Oh, dear lord, the bris," Grandmère murmured. "I'd forgotten."

"What's a bris?" Rocky asked loudly, but everyone shushed him for fear he'd wake the babies.

"You're sure you want to do this, Clarisse?" Helen Thermopolis asked Grandmère worriedly as the footmen loaded our luggage into the back of the limo.

"Because you don't have to go, you know. We could get all of you a set of rooms at the Ritz, or the Four Seasons. . . ."

"Don't have to go?" Grandmère tossed her head loftily. "I most certainly do. The national pride of Genovia rests upon my shoulders! I cannot allow the children's school to be defeated by The Royal Academy in Switzerland! We must win victory for the righteous."

I've never won victory for the righteous before. I'm not even completely sure what it means.

But I'm looking forward to finding out, I guess.

Wednesday, November 25
1:00 P.M.
Train to Stockerdörfl

I have to print really small because I don't want anyone to see what I'm writing in here. I told them all that I'm doing sketches of the beautiful country-side as it whizzes past us.

Ha! As if!

We changed trains at Genoa to a high-speed line (so we could get to Stockerdörfl in five hours instead of fourteen) and you can't see ANYTHING out the train windows—at least not for long enough to draw it—because we're going so fast.

But I *have* to write down all the crazy stuff that is happening.

NEVER GO ON A SCHOOL TRIP WITH YOUR GRANDMOTHER (AND YOUR SNOBBY COUSIN).

It will not turn out well.

It started out fine. I was excited because I've never been on a train before. Everywhere we've gone since I've found out I'm a princess has been on a private plane or in a limo. Before, when I lived in New Jersey, I never went anywhere, except by car.

I've *seen* lots of trains before—people took trains from New Jersey to get into Manhattan, and in Genovia people take trains to get all over the rest of Europe.

I didn't want to let on how excited I was to ride one—even more excited than Rocky, who loves everything with wheels, and even things with blades on them, as illustrated by his trying to hitch Snowball to a fake sleigh.

But I was SUPER EXCITED to ride on a train. Would it be, I kept wondering, like the train to Hogwarts, in Harry Potter?

But of course it wasn't. It was one of those modern trains—that Rocky went even *more* bananas for—not one with a smokestack. They don't use those anymore, because they cause too much pollution. I don't know what I'd been thinking.

And there were only three platforms at the train station, because Genovia isn't that big, and all the trains from there connect to other, bigger stations, where you can find the train going to where you want to go (such as Stockerdörfl).

But when I saw my entire class, practically, waiting for us on platform two, I got over my disappointment. Maybe this trip wouldn't be so bad.

Wrong. Very wrong.

"What is *she* doing here?" Luisa snarled upon spying my grandmother.

Fortunately she didn't say it loudly enough for Grandmère to overhear. If she had, I could only imagine what might have occurred. Possibly a third world war.

"My grandmother volunteered to chaperone," I said, keeping a tight hold on Snowball's leash. She was excited by all the new sights and smells at the train station. "And you should be thankful for it, Luisa, because if she hadn't, we wouldn't be able to—"

—*take this trip*, was what I was going to say, but I didn't get the chance to finish. That's because Victorine screamed out my name and began running toward me, throwing both her arms around my neck in a manner that caused my bodyguard, Serena, to reach for her stun gun.

That's because Victorine looks very different when she's not wearing her school uniform, and Serena didn't recognize her. After my sister's wedding, Victorine got super into the rock star Boris P, who played at the reception. So now when she's outside of school, Victorine dresses in all black, with very heavy black eyeliner and mascara, because she is a Borette—a Boris P fan.

"Oh my God, oh my God," Victorine cried. "We are going to have SO MUCH FUN! I'm so glad you're coming!"

After I'd extracted myself from Victorine's stranglehold, I said, "Um, I know—"

"What is going on here?" Grandmère demanded. "Why are you all out of uniform?"

Victorine spun around, saw my grandmother, then turned quite pale beneath her dark makeup. "Oh, good morning, Your Royal Highness," she said with a curtsy. "Madame Alain told us it was all right to wear our normal clothes on the train."

"Well, then I shall have a word with Madame Alain," Grandmère declared. "How are we to intimidate the enemy if we don't look like a united front? You there—" She yelled at Roger, the 12th Duke of Marborough, who was pointing at Rommel and laughing. "Do you find something amusing about my dog?"

Roger dropped his hand and stopped laughing. "No, ma'am—I mean, Your Highness."

"I should hope not. Just as there is nothing amusing about your shirt. Who, might I ask, is Tupac?"

"Uh," the duke said, looking down at his shirt, which featured a large portrait of the rap artist above his name and date of death. "He's, um, a . . . a philosopher, Your Highness."

"A philosopher. I see. Can you quote some of his writings?"

"Um . . ." The duke, who'd been helping Prince Khalil and some of the other members of the hockey team load equipment onto the train, looked startled. "What?"

"Don't say *what* to me, young man. Since you admire Mr. Tupac's philosophical writings so much that you feel compelled to wear the poor man's face emblazoned across your chest, I am assuming you can quote his writings."

The duke stared at my grandmother with a terrified expression. "Um . . ."

"If you'd like me to repeat the question, say 'I beg your pardon' or 'Excuse me,' but not 'um.'"

"Um . . . I don't think I . . ."

It was Prince Khalil who replied, "I can quote some of Tupac's writings, Your Highness."

Then he rapped, RIGHT ON THE TRAIN PLATFORM, the first few lyrics of a song by Tupac Shakur called "Dear Mama," which was about being respectful and appreciative of his mother, the woman who raised him and kept him from the penitentiary.

Everyone standing on the platform—me, Victorine, Nadia, Prince Gunther, Princess Komiko, Luisa, the Duke of Marborough, the Marquis of Tottingham, and the rest of the hockey team, and even some of the porters, and of course my bodyguard, Serena—all stared at him in admiration. The boy could sing!

"Dude," Roger said, when Prince Khalil was finished. "That was sweet!"

Prince Khalil lightly slapped the duke's raised hand. "No big thing," he said modestly.

"Yes," Grandmère agreed, after a moment's silence (except for the conductor, yelling for us to *Climb aboard!* since the train would soon be departing). "That *was* sweet." To the duke, she said, "Give him your shirt."

Roger's jaw dropped. "What?"

"You don't deserve to wear that shirt. A true fan

of Mr. Tupac would be able to quote him, as your friend did. So Prince Khalil deserves the shirt you are wearing, not you. Give it to him."

Prince Khalil looked shocked. "Your Highness," he said, "that's all right. I don't want the duke's—"

"Never fear," Grandmère said, holding out a hand to stop his protests. "The Duke of Marborough has plenty of other shirts, one presumes. He shan't go naked."

The duke wasn't the only person who was astonished. I was shocked, too.

"Grandmère," I said. "You can't—"

"I most certainly can," she said. "I am a chaperone. It's my duty not only to protect you, but to keep you from behaving in a way that might embarrass yourselves, or the reputation of the Royal Genovian Academy."

"But," Luisa cried, coming to the defense of the duke, who was—it couldn't be denied—the second most popular boy in our class, after Prince Khalil. If popularity was judged by how kind people were,

Prince Gunther would be second most popular. But for unknown reasons, this is not how popularity worked at the RGA. "Madame Alain is a chaperone, too. And she wouldn't want Roger to give up his shirt."

"Well, Madame Alain isn't here right now, is she?" Grandmère raised both her drawn-on eyebrows—a dangerous sign. "And I believe the right thing for the duke to do is stop pretending to be something he is not. That is neither impressive nor healthy. Hurry up now, young man. We haven't got all day. We've a train to board."

Roger looked from my grandmother to Luisa, rolled his eyes, then pulled off his Tupac shirt and tossed it to Prince Khalil.

"Here," he said, not very graciously.

"Uh." Prince Khalil looked down at the shirt. "Thanks . . . I guess."

I was mortified. It was one thing to deliver messages from the Resistance across the Austrian border to the Allies in Switzerland. It was another to enforce a completely unnecessary (and made-up) dress code. Was Grandmère going to be like this *the whole trip*?

Then Prince Khalil did something that completely distracted me from being mortified about my grandmother's crazy behavior:

He pulled off his own shirt so he could put on the duke's. Suddenly he—like the duke—was shirtless on platform two of the Genovian train station!

It was only for about four seconds or so.

But if you think about it, four seconds is a pretty

long time. Long enough for Prince Khalil to pull the duke's shirt over his head, and the duke to lean over and pull a new shirt from his backpack, and put it on, as well.

But it was also long enough for me to whip out my cell phone and take a really quick photo of a shirtless Prince Khalil for Nishi.

I *know* it was wrong, and something only a creepy, stalkery paparazzo would do.

But it wasn't my fault! Nishi's turned me into a creepy, stalkery paparazzo with her stupid bet (even though I'm the one who made the bet in the first place).

And she's the one who wanted a photo of Prince Khalil shirtless in the first place!

Well, now she's getting one. He just isn't smiling in front of a sunset, the way she wanted. He's changing his shirt on a train platform.

Nishi is going to have to learn to live with disappointment.

And to be fair, I *am* the school photographer for the trip. Taking photos is my job.

"Princess Clarisse!" Madame Alain cried as she returned to the platform from the train station's gift shop, where she'd gone to buy Genovian toffees for the trip. "What in heaven's name is going on here?"

"Nothing at all, Madame Alain," Grandmère replied calmly. "Merely a wardrobe adjustment. The Duke of Marborough generously volunteered to give the shirt off his back to the Prince of Qalif. But then, who would expect otherwise from the Duke of Marborough, who is such a charming and intelligent young man? Come, Madame Alain. I think the conductor would like us to board now."

"Oh." Madame Alain looked flustered. "Er . . . yes, Your Highness."

When we got on the train—the three first-class cars had been reserved by the Royal Genovian Academy for the fifty-seven students, ten chaperones, and fourteen bodyguards who'd be attending the school trip—I sat as far from Grandmère, Rommel, Madame Alain, and Rocky as I could possibly get, keeping Snowball on my lap. (Pets are allowed on European trains, within reason. For instance, you can't keep your pony on your seat with you, but you can take a small dog.)

After what had happened with the Duke of Marborough, I didn't think anyone would want to sit near me. I clearly had a crazy grandmother.

So you can imagine how surprised I was when Nadia and Princess Komiko plunked down beside me, followed by Victorine, and, finally, a slightly sullen Luisa.

"Oh my gosh," Victorine said, wiping tears of laughter from her eyes. "That was fantastic. 'A true fan of Mr. Tupac would be able to quote him.' I love your grandmother."

I peeked up from behind the powder-puff of white fur on Snowball's head. "You do?"

"Of course!" Victorine whipped out her cell phone to check her dark eye makeup. "She's completely right. I mean, no self-respecting fan of Boris P would wear one of his shirts and not know any of his songs. It's like, be a poser, why don't you?"

I'm not the biggest fan of Boris P (even though he

is a friend of my sister's). I'm more into Beyoncé (and Taylor Swift and Katy Perry, of course).

"Well, I thought your grandmother was rude, Olivia," Luisa said. "Roger was shirtless in front of the entire train station!"

"Yes, I noticed how bothered he was by that," Nadia said sarcastically. "And how closely you were observing his muscles, Lady Luisa."

Luisa turned bright red. "I wasn't!"

"Actually," said Princess Komiko, "you kind of were. I noticed it, too."

I hoped no one had noticed me taking a photo— or two—of Prince Khalil. But it didn't seem as if anyone had.

Luisa turned even redder. "I happen to have a boyfriend, you know."

"Then why aren't you sitting with him?" asked Nadia.

Luisa's eyes widened as she looked around the train car. "I . . . I was going to, but I can't seem to find him right now. . . ." She evidently hadn't even thought about sitting next to Prince Gunther for the two-hour ride to Genoa, where we would change to the high-speed train to Stockerdörfl.

"He's sitting in the other car," Nadia pointed out. "With the rest of the snowboarders. They're strategizing about how they're going to beat TRAIS."

"Well," Luisa said, sinking back into her seat, "I knew that. I was letting him have some alone time with his team. It's important for athletes to bond."

I don't know about the other girls, but I didn't believe her for a second. I think Nadia was right, and Luisa may have been cheating—with her eyes—on Prince Gunther with the Duke of Marborough.

I didn't want to make a big deal out of it, though. Then someone might bring up how I'd been snapping photos of Prince Khalil.

And like Nishi had said, we're in the seventh grade: no one is getting married.

So I changed the subject. I said, "You guys, let's make a get-well card for Marguerite. I feel sad that she's so sick and can't be here."

"Okay," they said, and whipped out their cell phones.

"No," I said. "A *real* get-well card. On paper."

I ripped a page from my notebook and folded it in half and drew a cartoon of all of us waving to Marguerite from the train. Since I didn't have any magic markers to color it in, Luisa donated some lip gloss, Nadia some sparkle nail polish, and Victorine some purple eye shadow.

The card looks quite beautiful, if I do say so myself—and it was a great way to change the subject from shirtless boys. We're going to mail it when we get to Stockerdörfl.

Riding on the train is actually a lot of fun. The scenery is beautiful—for a long time we were riding along the ocean, which was so blue, and we passed a number of castles.

Even better, a man came around with a trolley

full of food and drinks and asked, in a lovely British accent, "Savory or sweet?"

Victorine translated: "Do you want a salty snack, or a sweet snack?"

I said, "Both, please!"

That's how I want my life to be when I'm grown-up: savory but with plenty of sweet, too.

Wednesday, November 25
7:00 P.M.
Eis Schloss
Stockerdörfl, Austria

We're here! I can't believe we finally made it.

The 12th Duke of Marborough and the 17th Marquis of Tottingham put a smoke bomb down the toilet of the second first-class women's lavatory, causing it to explode and leaving us only one women's lavatory in our own car for the rest of the trip (and also causing Grandmère—as well as the train conductor—to want to throw the duke and the marquis off the train at the next stop).

Fortunately (or unfortunately) Madame Alain wouldn't let them. She said, "We can't leave the boys stranded in the middle of Italy!"

Finally she and the conductor compromised: The duke and the marquis could remain on the train, but only if they sat up in the first car by the driver's compartment with Madame Alain and Grandmère.

Grandmère said this was more of a punishment for her than the boys, but finally agreed.

The boys looked very sad sitting up there— Grandmère wouldn't let them play video games or text on their phones.

But who cares about them? Because now we're in Stockerdörfl! Which I have to say is living up to everything Prince Gunther has ever said about it. It really *is* a winter wonderland—a tiny medieval village tucked among the towering, snowy Alps. I guess in olden times, Prince Gunther's ancestors mined silver and copper from the mountains.

"But when the precious metals ran out," he told us proudly on the bus we took from the train to our hotel, "my great-great-great-grandfather Lapsburg von Stuben had the good idea to host a ski race for all the royals in Europe. And that is how Stocker-dörfl's reputation as the perfect place for ski vacations was born!"

I can see why Prince Gunther is so fond of his little town. It is very charming—even to someone like me, who can't ski.

And the place we are staying is one of the fanciest hotels I've ever been in . . . and I've stayed at the Plaza Hotel in New York City! It is called Eis Schloss. *Schloss* means castle or manor house. *Eis* means ice. Eis Schloss means Ice Castle (I guess).

Eis Schloss has:

- Two massive swimming pools (one indoor, one outdoor, both heated)

- Its own ski slopes (with lifts!)

- Ice-skating, sledding, and tubing

- Spa lounge and restaurant

- Fitness gym and studios

- Sauna with views of the mountains

- Steam bath with direct access to plunge pool

- Multiple restaurants and tea lounges

- Dog run for pets

I *really* think I'm going to like it here.

The only problem with it is that we have to share it with the other schools that are coming here for the Winter Games. We saw one of them—The Royal Academy in Switzerland—as we were checking in.

Now I understand why Grandmère wanted us to wear our uniforms on the train in order to intimidate them. The students from TRAIS looked much more professional in their red-and-white parkas and matching red-and-white snow pants than we did in our street clothes.

Not only that, but they were all much taller—and more muscular—than we are. I don't know what

the Swiss put in their food, but whatever it is, it seems to build much larger athletes than we're building in Genovia.

I didn't want to say anything to discourage our athletes, but judging on looks alone—and the way the TRAIS athletes lifted their noses at us in the lobby as they marched by—I'm pretty sure we're going to get creamed.

Oh well. At least our rooms—I'm sharing one with Nadia and Princess Komiko, since part of the Royal School Winter Games experience is learning how to get along with others—are nice. We even have our own coffeemaker (not that I drink coffee, but I've decided that I might start, since the coffee-maker comes with many fun differently flavored coffee packets, like Chocolate Mint and Toffee Mocha Dream).

We have to change for dinner now, which we're having in one of the Eis Schloss restaurants—the fondue one.

That's right: FONDUE.

I've never had fondue before. And I've certainly never had fondue in the *Alps* before.

I wanted to ask Prince Khalil if he'd ever had cheesecake dipped in chocolate fondue before (supposedly a delicacy).

But when I called his name, he was too busy talking to the rest of the hockey team to pay any attention.

It's true he was sitting kind of far away and things on the bus were very loud and maybe (like Princess Komiko has assured me) he didn't hear me calling his name.

But I think it's more possible that Prince Khalil is avoiding me now. Did he notice me taking a photo of him when he was shirtless on the train platform? If so, it's only natural that he'd be disgusted and want to avoid me. He doesn't know that it's only because I lost a bet.

This is why gambling is frowned upon and also illegal in many parts of the world.

And even if he doesn't know, the fact that my grandmother forced him to take the duke's shirt (although he could always give it back when Grandmère isn't looking. It's not like he HAS to keep it. So long as the duke doesn't wear it around Grandmère, it's fine) is probably reason enough to make him want to stay away from me.

Then again, what do I even care? Unlike Nishi, I'm not boy crazy. So if Prince Khalil doesn't like me anymore, it doesn't matter to me.

Except that it does . . . it *does* matter! Because I really do like Prince Khalil (as a friend), and I want him to like me.

I think that's part of my problem: I want *everyone* to like me! It's one of my worst qualities. I told my sister about it once, and she says she understands, because she feels the same way.

"If I give a speech to one hundred people," Mia said, "and ninety-nine of them say they loved the speech, but one person says he doesn't, all I can focus on is the one person who hated it. That's human nature, Olivia. We're all that way. We want everyone to love us. But that's impossible. We can't make everyone happy all the time. And the fact is, if we *are* making everyone happy all the time, we're probably not doing our jobs right. Because at some point, someone isn't going to get what they want. Someone has to lose."

Oh well. I have more important things to worry about right now than whether or not Prince Khalil likes me . . .

. . . such as the fact that Luisa and Victorine have the room right across the hall, and Victorine is banging on our door, making Snowball bark.

What could be wrong now?

DRAMA!

Luisa and Prince Gunther have had another one of their fights!

(Even though, according to the note Luisa gave me just yesterday, they "never fight" and are "totally and completely in love" in a way that I am too immature to understand.)

I don't know where they found the time to have a fight between our getting off the bus, checking into our hotel rooms, and getting ready for dinner.

But that's what Victorine was pounding on our door about.

"Luisa's in our room crying," Victorine said, looking upset. "She says Prince Gunther has broken her heart."

"What?" Nadia could hardly contain her glee. She loves gossip, and also anything to do with drama. I think this is left over from her being an actress and working on the soap opera back in her home country. *"Why?"*

"I don't know," Victorine said. "But I need your help. She can't go down to dinner crying like this. People will think there's something really wrong with her, and then they'll stare at us and come over and ask questions like *Is there anything we can do for you, little girl?* But we can't leave her alone, either, because she's threatening to do something to herself."

"Like *what*?" Nadia asked, her eyes nearly bursting out of her head.

"Like dye a purple streak in her hair."

Nadia looked disappointed. "Is that all?"

"Really," Princess Komiko said, "that's not so bad." She pointed at the purple streak in her own hair, which was a clip-on since she said her parents would kill her if she dyed her hair. "It might look good."

"I agree," I said. "Why can't we let her?"

"Because she isn't a Borette, like me," Victorine declared. Many fans of the rock singer Boris P have multicolored streaks in their hair. "Or a royal back in her home country, like Princess Komiko. Luisa could never pull it off. She doesn't have the confidence *or* the wardrobe. All of her clothes are designer."

Victorine was right. Luisa was probably only threatening to dye her hair to get attention, not because she really wanted a purple streak.

"Whatever we do, let's do it soon," Victorine said. "I'm starving."

I admired Victorine for being both compassionate and practical. Also, I was starving, too. It had been a long time since our savory and sweet snacks on the train (although I'd had four of them).

"Right," I said. "Let's go talk to her."

So we all piled into Victorine and Luisa's room, which was exactly like ours, except that it had one empty bed, where Marguerite would have slept if she hadn't come down with La Grippe.

Luisa looked great for someone who claimed her heart was broken. She'd changed into the clothes she was going to wear for dinner—Claudio jeans and a shimmery off-the-shoulder sweater, as well as faux-fur-lined boots—and her hair and makeup were perfectly in place. She simply couldn't seem to get up off the bed, across which she was sprawled, crying (although without any tears, I noticed, which was an impressive skill).

"H-he doesn't understand my needs," she sobbed as we all clustered around her and patted her on the back. "I texted that I need us to spend more time together, but he texted back that he had to stay with his parents, but that he'd see me at dinner."

"Well," I said, "Prince Gunther's parents *do* live in Stockerdörfl. They're hosting this whole event, and paying for a lot of it. So it sort of makes sense he'd be staying with them rather than here at the hotel."

"But how can they be more important to him than *me*?" Luisa raised her not-tearstained face to ask.

This was a hard question to answer. Should a boy's parents be more important to him than his girlfriend? I looked at Princess Komiko to see if she knew, but she only shrugged and fiddled around with the purple hooves of her unicorn backpack.

Nadia coughed. "In the soap opera that I worked on, there was a teenage boy character who had to be very kind to his father—even though he was an evil man with a weather-controlling machine—because if he wasn't kind to him, his father's secret assassins would have killed his girlfriend. And his mother and sisters. So maybe that's how it is with Prince Gunther's father."

Luisa blinked. "Do you think that's true?"

"Oh, yes," Nadia said, nodding. "Probably."

I highly doubted that Prince Gunther's father was going to have Prince Gunther's girlfriend killed if he didn't spend time with the family, but was happy to agree with anything that would get Luisa moving downstairs to dinner.

"I'm sure it's true," I said. "So you might want to be extra supportive of Prince Gunther while we're here."

"Yes," Luisa said with a sigh. "I suppose I should."

So now we're down in the fondue restaurant . . . but if this is what Luisa calls "being supportive," I'd hate to see how she treats someone she doesn't like.

The restaurant has a private room set up for us, with eight big tables with a grill in the middle of each, over which we're heating the different pots for our fondue sauces.

But instead of sitting at a table with Prince Gunther, Luisa walked *right by him* and plopped down at a table with the Duke of Marborough and the Marquis of Tottingham!

Prince Gunther looked like he was about to cry. "Luisa hates me," he said with the saddest sigh I'd ever heard.

"Oh, no," I said, glancing with alarm at my

friends. "Luisa doesn't hate you. She's just, uh, having a bad day."

Nadia, Princess Komiko, and Victorine all assured him that Luisa didn't hate him, as well.

But I don't think any of us did a very good job, because Prince Gunther continued to stare into the dancing flames of our fondue fire, looking as if he wished he were anywhere else but with us.

Then something incredible happened. Prince Khalil walked into the restaurant, looked around . . . and *headed straight for our table.*

Don't ask me why. It wasn't as if there weren't any seats available at the other tables, especially the ones where the cool people were sitting (there were).

"May I sit here?" he asked, indicating the empty chair beside mine.

Of course I said yes (or at least I think I did. I'm not entirely sure what came out of my mouth).

Prince Khalil sat down. I tried not to be too aware of how he smelled, which was clean and fresh. He had taken a shower (or maybe had a swim in the saltwater infinity pool) and changed from the Tupac shirt into a nice wool sweater.

I had never seen him in a sweater before. In Genovia, the weather is too warm for them. He looked very nice.

"What's the matter with *him*?" Prince Khalil asked me in a low voice, nodding at Prince Gunther.

"Oh," I said, in an equally low voice, "I think he and Lady Luisa are having a little bit of a disagreement." I didn't want to betray Luisa's trust—or Prince Gunther's—by going into too much detail.

"Oh." Prince Khalil held his menu in front of his face and pretended to be looking at the food selections, but really he was looking at Prince Gunther—and Luisa—from behind it. "Trouble in paradise, huh?"

I couldn't believe Prince Khalil was sitting next to me, casually gossiping, when he'd just ignored me on the bus!

Maybe he didn't hate me after all? Or maybe he really hadn't heard me when I'd called his name.

It was possible he hadn't seen me take that photo after all!

"Yeah," I said with a shrug. "Maybe."

"What's going on?" he asked. "She's mad but won't tell him why?"

"Um," I said. "Basically."

"I hate that kind of stuff," Prince Khalil said. "If something is on someone's mind, they should just tell the other person what it is. Games should be saved for the ice."

"Ha," I said. "Or the floating tennis table."

He grinned back at me. "Exactly."

I couldn't believe it! My plan—well, the plan Grandmère had suggested—was working. I was being kind to Prince Khalil, and he didn't look sad anymore.

He didn't know I'd secretly taken a photo of him with no shirt on and sent it to my best friend back in America as part of a bet, of course.

But that was going to stay my little secret (with Nishi).

Meanwhile, I was having fondue with him, and

it was going great. He knew exactly what to order, because he'd had fondue before—well, he and Prince Gunther had. So had Victorine. And Princess Komiko, actually. And Nadia.

Basically, I was the only person at the table who'd never had fondue before.

But that was okay, because all I had to do was watch what the others did and copy them. That's what Grandmère always said we should do when eating food with which we're not familiar (that and, if you found that you didn't like it, discreetly lay down your dining utensil and say that it turned out you'd had a huge lunch and weren't that hungry after all).

I didn't need to do that with fondue, though, because it was so good! We had the kind where you dipped pieces of bread into a big pot of warm, melty cheese, and then the chinoise kind—which was where you cooked the meat and vegetables in a pot of broth right at your table, and then shared the broth afterward as a soup—and then, for dessert afterward, the best kind of fondue of all . . .

Chocolate!

And even though there wasn't cheesecake, there were strawberries and pineapple and marshmallows and banana and it was *so* delicious and fun to huddle around the pot of creamy warm chocolate, especially since it was so cold outside, it had started *snowing*. You could see the big white soft flakes coming down outside the huge picture windows, which made it especially "jolly"—to use Prince Gunther's word— to be so snug and toasty inside.

Prince Khalil kept cracking me up, too, saying, "Oh, *excuse* me," in a goofy voice every time our long forks accidentally crossed inside the pot.

I wasn't the only one laughing, of course. Nadia and Victorine and Princess Komiko and even Prince Gunther laughed, too.

But somehow I felt as if Prince Khalil's silly jokes were meant for me.

Ugh! Simply writing that, I realize how dumb I sound.

Don't worry, though. It didn't go on for very long. Because we weren't the only ones staying at Eis

Schloss who had reservations for La Fondue that night. It turned out that the British Aristocracy Training School, or BrATS, and also the French Academy of Royals (FARs) had reservations right after ours, so our chaperones for the night—Madame Alain, Monsieur Chaudhary, and Mademoiselle Justine—kept trying to hurry us along.

"Eat up, eat up, Your Highnesses," Mademoiselle Justine kept calling out. "We must be done with our cheese course in *douze minutes*! *Douze minutes*, my lords and ladies!"

There's nothing more annoying than being told you have twelve minutes to do something . . . except maybe someone going over a schedule while you're doing something else.

But that's what Madame Alain decided to do. Which was hand out, and then explain—in excruciating detail—the schedule for the next two days. Which is how:

A. I have so much time to be writing all this . . . I look like I'm taking notes. And I am . . . sort of!

B. I found out that as school photographer, I'm

supposed to be EVERYWHERE AT ALL TIMES tomorrow. Although Madame Alain strongly encourages *all of us* to try to go to every event in which we are not participating, so that we can cheer for our teammates.

But I guess I shouldn't complain, since at least I'll get all those other photos Nishi wanted . . . and I won't even have to make up an excuse to tell Prince Khalil about why I'm taking a picture of him: Taking pictures of him (and everyone else) is my job for the next couple of days!

Maybe while I'm taking photos of Prince Khalil for Nishi, I'll take a couple for myself. You know, just to keep, and not hand in to the yearbook committee or school paper.

HA HA! JUST KIDDING. I'm not a stalker.

I don't think.

But I did notice while we were sharing all those fondue pots together that Prince Khalil's eyes *are* awfully big and soft and brown looking.

Almost as big and soft and brown-looking as Snowball's.

Wait . . . is it weird to compare a boy's eyes to your dog's? I think it is.

I'm weird. They should change my name from Princess Olivia to Princess Weird.

Oh well. I DON'T CARE!!!

WEDNESDAY November 25	THURSDAY November 26	FRIDAY November 27
ARRIVAL	Speed Skating 08:30 500m Boys 08:30 500m Girls	Ice Hockey Finals Boys 08:00 ___ vs ___
	Ice Hockey Boys 09:00 FARs vs. RGA 11:00 BrATS vs. TRAIS	Ice Hockey Finals Girls 09:00 ___ vs ___
	Ice Hockey Girls 10:00 BrATS vs. RGA 12:00 FARs vs. TRAIS	Figure Skating 10:00 Finals Boys 10:00 Finals Girls
	Cross-Country Skiing 11:00 Classic Boys 11:00 Classic Girls	Snowboarding 11:00 Finals Boys 11:00 Finals Girls
	Ski-Jumping 12:00 Girls 12:00 Boys LUNCH	LUNCH and Medals Ceremony
	Dogsledding 14:00	
	Figure Skating 15:00 Semis Boys 15:00 Semis Girls	
	Snowboarding 16:00 Semis Boys 16:00 Semis Girls	

HRH Princess Mia Thermopolis "FtLouie"

Hi, Olivia! Just checking in to see how things are going in Stockerdörfl. I hope you aren't too cold up there in the mountains! Do you have enough sweaters? How are you feeling? Is your throat sore at all? What about Rocky? Has anyone asked if you want to build a snowman? ☺ ☺ ☺ Just kidding. Send photos!

We're fine (in case you're worrying) and so are the babies. They miss their aunt Olivia, though! I'm so, so sorry that Dr. Khan sent you away, but I'm sure it's for the best. And they say that La Grippe is already on the wane. Fewer cases were reported today than any day all week.

Say hello to Rocky and Snowball for us. Oh, and Grandmère, too. I hope she's letting you have fun!

XOXOX Mia

P.S. I almost forgot—a letter arrived for you the day before you left. It has the royal crest of Qalif on it. The Royal Genovian Press Office should have forwarded it to you as soon as it arrived, but as you know, a lot has been going on over the past couple of days! 😉

Anyway, I think it's probably a birthday card from your aunt. Do you want me to throw it out? I'm happy to do so if you want me to. You know you don't have to communicate with those people ever again if you don't want to.

Let me know what you want to do.

XOXOX Mia

P.P.S. You still haven't told us what you want for your birthday! I know things have been busy, but there isn't much time left. Can you give us a little hint, at least?

☺ ☺ ☺ XOXO

P.P.P.S. Sorry this is so long.

Oh my gosh. I totally forgot—I'm an aunt!

I feel so guilty. I've been so caught up in the drama around here, I completely forgot about the new babies!

But if they'd been my responsibility, I wouldn't have forgotten. Snowball is my responsibility, and I haven't forgotten about *her*. I've been feeding her and taking her for walks (even though it's about thirty degrees outside and there's a foot of fresh snow on the ground, so I have to put her little snow booties on so she doesn't get ice chunks between her toes). I'm making sure she gets plenty of fresh water and lots of cuddles. I'm a good dog mother!

And if I were home with the twins, I'd be a good aunt to them, too.

Not like *my* aunt, who apparently suddenly remembered my existence.

I'm kind of not surprised. She and her family moved to Qalif—where they wanted to take me, too, until Mia and Dad stopped them.

I guess I did sort of forget she was living there. Probably she isn't sending me happy birthday wishes at all, but writing to ask for money so she can move back to New Jersey. I can't imagine she'd want to live in a place where there is a civil war going on.

Well, fat chance! She stole all the money Dad was sending her to take care of me. She can use that to get out of Qalif.

But who has time to worry about *that* drama when there is so much more exciting drama here???

It started after dinner, when we all went to our rooms (Madame Alain said it was important for us to get plenty of sleep tonight, since the Games would begin tomorrow morning right after our buffet breakfast downstairs, and we needed to be fresh if we were going to decimate the competition).

Princess Komiko and I were brushing our teeth in the bathroom when we heard a *THUD* against the glass doors to the balcony.

"What was *that*?" Nadia cried.

Even though we were all in our pajamas, we rushed out onto the balcony to look . . .

. . . and got pelted with snowballs.

"Ha ha," cried some voices from down below us.

"Stupid Genovians! They have never seen snow before! They are so dumb, they won't know what to do!"

I had so much snow in my face, I couldn't see where it was coming from.

But Nadia, who had been in the bedroom when the first snowball hit the balcony door, had gotten a good look at the perpetrators.

"I saw red," she hissed from behind the table where we'd ducked. "Red-and-white tracksuits!"

Princess Komiko gasped. "The Royal Academy in Switzerland!"

"That's it," I said, grabbing some snow off one of the balcony's chairs and forming it into a ball. "THIS IS WAR!"

So that's what we've been doing all night. It's TRAIS against the RGA!

We sent an emergency text to everyone in the hotel (who attends the Royal Genovian Academy, of course) about what is happening.

I know that technically we're all in school to learn diplomacy.

But when someone hits you in the face with a

ball of snow, all diplomacy goes out the window. Er, balcony door. It's time to FIGHT!

Besides, Serena has really good aim (of course she's joined in. She can't allow me to be struck by enemy fire, even if it is only a snowball).

From the seventh grade, we've managed to get Prince Khalil, Princess Komiko, Nadia, Victorine, Luisa, the 12th Duke of Marborough, and the 17th Marquis of Tottingham on our side.

(Okay, I'm not too thrilled about the last two, but we really need all the help we can get. I mean, even *Rocky* is here making snowballs for us to throw. He's stacking them up behind the sun loungers we've overturned and are using as our fort and home base down by the infinity pool.)

I'm wearing my snow boots, puffy vest, neck warmer, and mittens over my pajamas. I sincerely hope there are no paparazzi around, because if they get a photo of me running around the hotel like this, Grandmère is going to give me her "I'm very disappointed in you, Olivia" speech.

But it will be worth it.

Thursday, November 26
1:30 A.M.
Eis Schloss
Stockerdörfl, Austria

I'm writing this in the bathroom because my room-
mates are in bed with the lights out and I don't want
to disturb them . . . but I know I'll never get to sleep
if I don't get this down!

Two of the weirdest things just happened. One
was good—I think—and one was bad.

Really, *really* bad.

Good Thing first:

Prince Khalil told me that I look cute!!!!

It's true.

The bad part is—well, one of the bad parts—he said it as we were all going inside after the snowball fight, which got busted BY MY GRANDMOTHER.

I already knew from the T-shirt incident on the train platform that having Grandmère as a chaperone was going to be tricky.

But I didn't think she wasn't going to let us have any fun at all!

(Although I will admit, things did get a little out of hand when kids from both BrATS and FARs showed up. I think there might have been people who weren't even part of the Royal School Winter Games throwing snowballs. I'm pretty sure I spotted a few of the hotel employees hurling a couple at us.)

All of it came to an end, however, when Grandmère came storming out of the hotel in her bathrobe, nighttime turban, and boots, and yelled (in French), "Cease this behavior at once, Your Royal Highnesses, or *I will telephone your parents*!"

I have no idea whose parents she meant . . . she might actually have meant everyone's parents. I'm pretty sure she knows all their parents, because I

saw Grandmère's Rolodex once (that's an old-timey thing that people used to use in the days before address books on cell phones), and it is HUGE. It takes up her entire desk, practically.

Anyway, everyone was so scared after that (I think mostly of the turban) that they dropped their snowballs and started going back inside, including me. I pretended like I didn't know who Grandmère was.

Don't get me wrong. I love her, and everything.

But I'm super hoping she didn't notice me in the crowd (she didn't give any sign that she did) because I do not want to get one of her speeches about how "disappointed" she is in me, and how my behavior might reflect badly on the crown.

Anyway, it was as all this was happening that the 17th Marquis of Tottingham looked at me and started laughing.

"Renaldo," he said, "you should see yourself right now. You look even more like an alien than your grandma!"

Great. What a lovely end to what had otherwise been a fun evening, I thought. Who wouldn't enjoy being told she looked like an alien by the 17th Marquis of Tottingham?

And to make it worse, I didn't know what he was talking about. I couldn't see myself, because even though there were large gilt-framed mirrors all over the lobby, I was wearing my glasses, and the lenses had gotten steamed up as we'd come in from the cold (I think that's what Tots meant by calling me an alien).

I don't think people like the 17th Marquis of Tottingham, who has twenty-twenty vision, understand the challenges faced by those of us who don't, and how, if you have to wear glasses, sometimes when you step suddenly from a very cold environment into a very warm one, they are so fogged up, you can't see a thing!

And yes, I *know* I could just get contacts.

But I am not ready yet for the responsibility of sticking things INTO MY EYES.

So of course I rushed over to the elevators—where there are some especially large mirrors—to see how bad I looked (after I'd cleaned off my lenses on my pajama sleeve). I mean, you never knew: Tots could have been referring to something other than my crazily fogged-up glasses. I am not a super-vain person (in my opinion), but if my hair was looking deformed, I at least wanted to be able to do some damage control before anyone else saw it (not that I care particularly what Tots thinks. I was actually thinking about sneaking back outside and grabbing some more snow and stuffing it down the front of Tots's coat).

That's when Prince Khalil said it. He said, "Cut it out, Tots. I think Princess Olivia looks cute."

I think Princess Olivia looks cute.

Just like that. IN FRONT OF EVERYONE.

Of course, he could have been saying it because that's the kind of thing princes are supposed to say. And the kind of thing they are supposed to be: charming. We go to a school that trains us in good manners and social graces *every day*.

But it's possible he was saying it for other reasons . . . like, you know, that he *really does think I'm cute*.

That's what Nadia thinks, anyway, *and* Princess Komiko. Because they heard him say it, both elbowed me afterward and raised their eyebrows, like, "Oooooh!" causing me to want to pull my neck warmer up over my entire face in embarrassment.

Not that I care what Prince Khalil thinks.

Very much.

"Ha ha," I said nervously, stabbing at the up button on the elevator, hoping this would make the doors open faster and I could run away. "Um . . . thanks, Your Highness."

(Because you have to thank someone when they pay you a compliment, even if it's just a compliment that they said because someone was picking on you and they felt sorry for you or whatever.)

But of course pushing the button for the elevator a million times didn't make it come any faster.

And because the elevator didn't come, I was there for the Bad Thing to happen. Well, the other bad thing besides the fact that my grandmother had come down from her room in her night turban and bathrobe to yell at us for having a snowball fight.

The Bad Thing didn't happen to me. I only *saw* it happen. I haven't told anyone . . . yet. To be honest, I don't know what to do about it—it's so gross and unbelievable and sad and yet kind of exciting (only not in a good way) all at the same time.

As I was pushing the up button, I glanced into the mirrors on either side of the elevator to check my hair one last time (it looked perfectly normal).

That's when I saw it: Luisa leaning against the far wall of the lobby, over by the large open fireplace, being kissed by a tall, blond boy. . . .

GROSS! Public displays of affection much? Good thing Grandmère had apparently grabbed a different elevator and gone back upstairs already.

But wait . . . the tall, blond boy kissing Lady Luisa wasn't Prince Gunther. He'd gone home for the night.

It was *the 12th Duke of Marborough*!

I couldn't believe it. I mean, I know Luisa and Prince Gunther haven't exactly been getting along lately.

But when had *this* happened?

As soon as I saw the duke's face, I must have gasped or something, because Nadia, who was standing right next to me, asked, "Princess Olivia? Are you all right?"

"Fine. I'm fine," I said, and jabbed at the elevator button some more. "Oh my gosh, what is taking this thing so long?"

I could see in the reflection in the mirror that

behind me, Luisa and the duke were now holding hands and whispering into each other's ears.

Luisa, I groaned inwardly. *How could you be so dumb?*

Because if *I'd* seen what Luisa was doing, other people could, too. Which meant that eventually, even though Prince Gunther had gone home for the night, someone who'd seen what was going on was going to tell him about it.

And then Prince Gunther was going to be *so* hurt! Even though he was weird, that didn't mean Prince Gunther didn't have feelings.

It was fine if Luisa didn't want to go out with him anymore. I could understand that. There's a reason why in most countries (though not all) it's illegal for people under the age of eighteen to get married or sign any kind of legal contract: Young people change their minds *a lot*, because their minds are still growing (some at different rates than others).

But Luisa could at least have the common decency

to break up with Prince Gunther before *literally* kissing someone else behind his back!

Especially someone like the 12th Duke of Marborough, who is (in my opinion, anyway) a jerk and a show-off.

"Oh, phew," I said with exaggerated relief as the elevator doors finally opened with a pinging sound. "The elevator is here!"

I yelled it very loudly so that Luisa would hear me, and know I was there, and maybe stop what she was doing.

I don't know if she took the hint, since I hopped onto the elevator with everyone else and rode to my floor (the girls from the RGA are on the third floor, the boys on the fourth).

As I got out, Prince Khalil said, "Good night!"

But I think he said it more generally to everyone getting out on my floor (me, Victorine, Princess Komiko, Nadia, Snowball, and some of the senior girls) than only to me.

I said "good night" back, though, and watched as the elevator doors closed on his face. (Well, okay, not *on* his face. He wasn't squished to death by the elevator doors. You know what I mean.)

But now I'm left with the terrible memory of what I saw.

Not of Prince Khalil's face being squished by the elevator doors. Of my cousin kissing the duke.

Seeing my cousin kiss anyone would be disgusting. But seeing her kiss the 12th Duke of Marborough?

I don't know how I'm ever going to be able to get to sleep. I probably have post-traumatic stress from it (post-traumatic stress is something my sister, Mia, talks about a lot. She says she has it from high school).

And it's not even like we were playing spin the bottle (which Nadia suggested we do tomorrow night, because apparently on an episode of the soap opera she was in, some of the kids did that. YUCK. No, no, no, and NO).

Oh well. Maybe I'll just try not to think about Luisa. Maybe I'll try to think about the Good Thing that happened to me instead:

Prince Khalil said I'm cute.

Nadia says he *definitely* likes me.

But Victorine says not to get my hopes up because last year at the Royal School Winter Games, Prince Khalil hung out the whole time with a redheaded girl named Princess Sophie Eugenie who is on the French Academy of Royals (FARs) girls' hockey team.

"And from what I hear, they're still texting," Victorine told me. "So if Sophie's here this year, the chances of him even noticing you're in the room instead are, like, zero . . . unless of course you suddenly take up hockey."

What is so great about hockey? That is what I'd like to know.

Table tennis is a far more challenging sport, and you can play it anywhere, even in a pool.

When I saw Luisa this morning at the breakfast buffet, she was acting like *nothing had happened.*

Seriously! She was sitting there holding Prince Gunther's hand (he came over from his house to have breakfast with her). She was innocently eating her yogurt and fruit like *she hadn't kissed the 12th Duke of Marborough (on the lips) in the lobby last night at all.*

Nadia and Princess Komiko kept asking me what

was wrong, but I only shook my head and said, "Nothing."

But something was wrong, all right. Something was VERY wrong.

Not with the food, though. Prince Gunther had assured all of us that Stockerdörfl has the best breakfasts in the world, and I will confess that I didn't believe him, because Chef Bernard back at the palace in Genovia makes the best waffles I've ever tasted.

But I have to say, Eis Schloss does have a pretty impressive breakfast buffet, and they set it up all along the picture windows in front of the mountain view, so it kind of takes your breath away (when you aren't staring at your cousin who is cheating on her very nice boyfriend who is the prince of the area in which you are currently staying).

But even though I was very impressed by the lovely breakfast buffet, and ate as much of it as my stomach would allow (which turned out to be a lot), all I could really do during the meal was stare at Luisa and think about how mean she was being to Prince Gunther.

Probably this makes me exactly what she says I am: a stick.

But I don't care. If sticks are loyal to their boyfriends and don't go around kissing dukes behind their backs, then I AM PROUD TO BE A STICK.

Finally Princess Komiko, Nadia, and Victorine got up to go. Madame Alain said it was a good idea to get to all events at least fifteen minutes early if we wanted to get good seats.

I knew what I had to do. As the Princess of Genovia (well, one of them), it's my duty to keep peace and tranquility in my native land.

And it's even MORE important to make sure that citizens of my country don't embarrass us by acting like total twits while we're visiting foreign lands.

So when I saw Prince Gunther get up to go refill his coffee cup—of *course* he drinks coffee, even though he's only thirteen, and not even with tons of sugar and milk; he drinks it black—I knew it was my chance to confront Luisa about her behavior. She was still sitting at their table, checking her lip gloss in the camera on her cell phone.

I was just heading over to Luisa's table when Grandmère swooped in—there is really no better word to describe how Grandmère enters a room than "swoop."

And it was especially pronounced today since she was dressed in a long fur coat with a matching fur hat, even though both my sister, Mia, and I have told her numerous times that it's tacky to wear fur unless you live in the Arctic or wearing fur is part of your indigenous culture (Grandmère says it is—"Dowager princesses are expected by the populace to wear fur and I can't disappoint them").

Anyway, Grandmère saw me and immediately swooped toward me, sat down across from me, ordered a hot water with lemon from one of the waitstaff, and said, "What is the matter with you? You look the way I did when I was a young debutante and couldn't find any stockings to wear to my coming-out party because of the worldwide silk shortage after the War."

I thought of telling her about what Luisa was doing to Prince Gunther, and how I intended to confront Luisa about it.

But telling on your cousin to your grandmother was something a stick-in-the-mud would do (or at least something Luisa would *expect* someone who was a stick-in-the-mud to do).

So instead I said, "I'm just a little concerned about something."

Grandmère narrowed her eyes. "Hmph. I wonder what. It couldn't have anything to do with that snowball battle I was forced to break up last night, could it? Oh yes," she added when I shook my head, trying to act as if I had no idea what she was talking about, "I know you were there. I heard all about your part in it this morning from my good friend Herr Schultz, the concierge of this fine establishment.

I have spies everywhere, you know, Olivia. Your grandmother knows all."

Oh no! She was going to give me her "I'm very disappointed in you, Olivia" speech! I wanted to crawl under the table in shame.

"Grandmère, I'm sorry. But if you'd heard the things those boys from The Royal Academy in Switzerland said about us, you'd have—"

"It is our duty, Olivia, as Princesses of Genovia, to set a good example while in a foreign country, and not act like hooligans—no matter how tempted by the poor behavior of others."

I hung my head. I knew she was right—even though of course it had been a lot of fun to act like a hooligan, and Prince Khalil had said I'd looked cute while doing it.

"You're right, Grandmère. I really am sorry."

"It's not me you should be apologizing to. You disturbed the other guests, and Herr Schultz said you created a great mess on the pool deck. There were footprints as well as discarded energy drink cans and protein bar wrappers everywhere. And one of your little friends even managed to knock down the hotel's ice sculpture of the Venus de Milo. It took the artist almost six hours to create that! And what kind of role model were you being for Rocky? He could have been injured."

"But he wasn't," I pointed out.

"Of course not," Grandmère said. "It's far more likely he hurt someone else. That is not the point. The point, Olivia, is that you come from a line of great female leaders. Even though you yourself will most likely never inherit the throne, you must act like one who rules at all times. And hurling snowballs at your adversaries is not the way a ruler behaves."

I thought about this. "But you basically said you shot at the Nazis when you were here during World War Two."

Both of Grandmère's eyebrows rocketed skyward, and I knew I was in big, big trouble.

"First of all, Olivia, the Nazis were an evil foreign entity who invaded our country—among many others—and killed millions of innocent people. They were not a rival school against whom we were competing in some winter games. And secondly, what I said was that I did much worse than shoot at them; your grandfather—my husband—did shoot at them, and was shot by them in return, and spent many months, even years, recovering from that wound. I chose a different path. I used the wits with which I was born, the social graces I learned in school, and the winter sports skills I learned at these Games to deliver a message I believe helped end the war a little sooner. What I am suggesting is that in the future you employ those same skills if you want to win— not just at these Games but at life in general."

I swallowed. I had only the vaguest idea what she was talking about. "Okay, Grandmère. Thanks for the advice. It sounds . . . good."

Meanwhile, over her shoulder, I could see that Prince Gunther had returned to the table he was sharing with Luisa, and she fed him a grape. Really! She was hand-feeding him grapes, like he was a monkey in the zoo or something!

"Well, I hope you will follow it." Grandmère shook her head. "Lord knows your sister rarely did. And look at the mess she's in now."

I wanted to point out that Mia didn't PLAN to have twins—it just HAPPENED that way, like in the movie *The Parent Trap*.

But then Grandmère's hot water with lemon arrived, and she accepted it with a gracious "*Danke*" to the waiter.

Grandmère says drinking hot water with lemon every morning cleans out the digestive system and helps with one's complexion.

I've tried it, and it works. Well, I don't know about the digestive tract, but I don't have any wrinkles.

But I'm probably going to have a massive stress breakout if I have to keep looking at what I saw on my way to the speed-skating competition, which was Luisa and Prince Gunther, holding hands. That pretty much made me want to throw up everything I had for breakfast.

Thursday, November 26
1:00 P.M.
Ski Lift to Beginner Slope

It's kind of hard to write in your journal when you're on a ski lift, but fortunately it's a sunny day, so it's actually kind of warm (as long as you don't accidentally move into a shady area; then it is freezing), so I took my gloves off. I had to get this all down before I forget:

First of all, I have SO MANY PHOTOS of Prince Khalil. Nishi better not complain that I haven't fulfilled the bet!

I covered both the girls' and boys' hockey games for the school paper, and got about a million photos of Prince Khalil (the Royal Genovian Academy beat the French Academy of Royals).

True, he had his helmet and pads on, but you could definitely tell it was him. He was even smiling in a few of them (with his mouth guard in).

Nishi should be very, very happy.

I haven't heard from her yet, but that's probably because it's still early in the US.

I wonder how things are going with Dylan, and if she's still getting a bad grade in English.

I got a few shots of Princess Sophie Eugenie, too (the girl who Victorine says Prince Khalil has been texting all year).

She's pretty, I guess—it's hard to tell with her goalie equipment on—but no big deal, if you ask me. I doubt she could draw a kangaroo.

Anyway, that isn't even what I want to write about. What I want to write about is why I'm on a ski lift:

I SKIED!

Yes, I skied. At lunchtime, after covering all the events, Prince Gunther saw me and yelled, "Renaldo!"

(Seriously. That's what everyone calls me now. Thanks, Tots. Although I guess it's better than Stick.)

"Um," I said. "Yes?"

"Have you learned to ski yet?" Prince Gunther asked.

"Not exactly."

To tell the truth, I was more scared to learn than ever, because I'd seen all the people coming down from the slopes near the hotel, and they were going super fast.

Also, the Alps are no joke. Some of them are made from *glaciers*. Although, as Mia explained to me at breakfast before I left, 30 to 40 percent of the Alpine glaciers in Austria and Switzerland have disappeared in the past one hundred years due to global warming. Something has to be done, which is why she's on a special committee at the UN to try to improve energy efficiency worldwide (but of course she hasn't been to any of the meetings lately, due to having been confined to her bed with the babies).

"Then I must teach you to ski!" Prince Gunther cried. "You cannot come to Stockerdörfl and not learn to ski!"

"Uh," I said. "That's okay. Really."

I mean, honestly, I would be okay going through my whole life never learning how to ski. I kind of like the fondue eating and sitting by the fire parts of ski resorts better than the skiing part.

But then I saw the disappointment on Prince Gunther's face. I knew how much he wanted me to enjoy his town, and remembered how Luisa was treating him (behind his back).

So I said, "Fine. I'll try it."

Prince Gunther's cry of happiness was so loud that it attracted the attention of several people from our class, including Princess Komiko and Prince Khalil, who were both already wearing skis from having taken a few "practice runs" down the intermediate slopes. They skied over with a coolness I felt pretty confident I would never acquire.

"What's going on?" Prince Khalil asked as he came swooshing to a stop.

"Princess Olivia has agreed to try to ski," Prince Gunther cried. "And I am going to teach her!"

"This I have got to see," Prince Khalil said.

I couldn't help noticing that, when Prince Gunther had said I'd agreed to ski, Prince Khalil's eyes seemed to have lit up.

At least I think they had. It was hard to tell behind his tinted ski goggles.

So all that was left was for me to get fitted with a pair of skis and boots (I wanted to try snowboarding, but Prince Gunther said it was better for beginners to learn downhill or alpine skiing first, then move up to snowboarding later if they still wanted to).

The ski boots felt VERY strange and huge on my feet, but Prince Gunther said that was because they were rented.

Francesca had warned me that this would happen, and had said we should buy me my own pair before I left, but Dad said not to be ridiculous, that he wasn't wasting money on something I wasn't even sure I would like.

This had caused Mia to ask sarcastically, "You mean like that race car you bought yourself, Dad?" which had caused Helen to burst out laughing, though Dad said indignantly, "That was different."

Prince Gunther and the others took me to something called a bunny slope, which is for beginners to practice on.

But honestly it still seemed pretty high to me, and at first I was scared.

Prince Gunther was a really good teacher, though, very patient and kind, just like he is about everything.

"You aren't going to fall down the mountain," he kept saying when I asked if that was something that could happen. "You see? First you would reach the town square. You would ski into the coffeeshop. And if you are going too fast, you can always point your skis together like I showed you. That is how you slow down."

"Or just fall over onto your butt," Princess Komiko suggested. "You can always stop that way."

"If you're a baby," Victorine said with a sneer. But it was a friendly sneer. She'd come along to watch, too. Everyone had come along to watch, it seemed, the spectacle of Princess Olivia learning how to ski . . .

. . . including Prince Khalil, who hasn't shown one sign—that I've noticed—of texting Princess Sophie Eugenie. He's been supporting me, too.

I've fallen down several times, but I don't care. In order to succeed, you have to fail. Anyone who doesn't know that has never tried anything before.

That pretty much describes my cousin Luisa, who is the only person from the seventh grade—I've noticed, with the exception of the 12th Duke of Marborough— who didn't come watch me learn how to ski. Victorine said they'd decided they were hungry and went back to the hotel to have lunch.

And Prince Gunther still doesn't suspect a thing! He is the most trusting person on the face of the planet . . .

a lot like my dog, Snowball, who will run up to anyone for a pat on the head, even people with much bigger dogs, or people who don't like dogs, or are allergic to them (like Luisa).

Snowball, like Prince Gunther, *especially* loves Luisa.

Fortunately I saw Grandmère heading in the same direction as Luisa and the duke. (Grandmère promised to watch Snowball while I ski. She barks too much when I do things she thinks are dangerous.)

Whatever Luisa and the duke are up to, Grandmère will hear about it from Herr Schultz, the concierge.

Anyway, so I'm not the best skier in the world.

But I'm good enough to graduate from the bunny slope, Prince Gunther says!

Which is why I'm on a ski lift (not alone. Serena is with me! I'm not stupid or anything. Serena is a champion skier. She trained in Zermatt with the National Women's Team of Israel).

I feel especially bad about what my cousin is doing to Prince Gunther now that he's been so nice to me and taught me to ski and all. He has NO idea what's going on, and is off skiing on the more difficult slopes with Prince Khalil, Princess Komiko, Victorine, Nadia, and Tots, totally oblivious to the fact that his heart is about to be broken.

I just asked Serena if she thinks I should say something to Prince Gunther about his girlfriend (since she was there last night, and saw the same thing I saw), and she said, "I'm sorry, Your Highness, but that question is above my pay grade."

Serena says she is only here to protect me from getting kidnapped or killed, not to give me relationship advice.

Which is a bummer because, based on how often her cell phone pings, I have the feeling Serena knows a lot about the complexities of the human heart.

Thursday, November 26
2:30 P.M.
Dogsledding Event

Oh my gosh!

Right after I wrote that last entry, I got to the top of the ski lift and realized I'd missed my stop.

Instead of getting off at the green slope (for beginners), I rode all the way up to the black diamond (most advanced—and dangerous!) because I was too engrossed in writing in my notebook!

And Serena had been too engrossed in texting with my sister about what to get me for my birthday to notice, either.

Serena said, "This is a gross dereliction of my duty, Princess. You could easily have been struck by an assassin's bullet while I wasn't paying attention. I am tendering my resignation as soon as we get down the mountain."

But I said, "No, Serena. Please don't resign. You're my favorite bodyguard and I would be lost without you. You're also the only person who can beat me at table tennis."

(It's true. Although everyone else might just be letting me win. Serena would never think of letting anyone beat her at anything.)

Serena agreed not to resign (for now).

But that didn't solve the problem of how I was going to get down from that slope.

Serena wanted to go ask the ski lift operator if we could ride down on the lift instead of skiing down, but I wouldn't let her. I said it would be too mortifying. Only babies, old ladies, and people from America who've been writing in their journals or overestimated their athleticism do that.

"But it's my job to protect you, Princess," Serena said.

"Yes," I said. "But not just my physical body. You have to help me protect my pride, too."

"Well then," Serena said, lowering her purple ski goggles. "Looks like we don't have any alternative, Your Highness. Come on. If we stay out of other people's way, zigzag, and take it slow, I think you can do it."

I looked down the slope. I'm not normally scared of heights, but this was ridiculous. The slope looked like a giant waterfall made of pure ice. It careened straight down into the center of downtown Stockerdörfl.

And people were expected to slide down that on two tiny pieces of wood?

But tons of people were doing it, flitting this way and that on it, like little brightly colored butterflies.

I'm no butterfly, though. I'm a human girl.

This was it. I was going to die.

"Okay," I said. I lowered my ski goggles, too. "Here we go. This is going to be great!"

I had no idea I was screaming until an extremely tall man and woman in bright orange ski suits glided over from the restaurant.

"Ladies," said the man. He had hair that was so blond, it was almost white. "Is something the matter? May I be of any assistance?"

"No," Serena said coldly, fingering the Taser strapped to her thigh. "We're fine."

"We're so fine," I cried. "I got off at the wrong slope. But I can ski down that hill! I just skied today for the first time ever and I can totally ski down that hill!"

"Oh," the lady said, laughing. "You poor thing. Don't worry, it happens all the time."

She couldn't pronounce the letter *w*, so the word "worry" came out *vorry*.

"Are you here for the Royal School Winter Games?" she asked.

"Yes," I said. "I'm Princess Olivia Grace Clarisse Mignonette Harrison Renaldo of Genovia, and this is my Royal Genovian Guard, Serena Yehoshua."

The woman and the man both looked surprised . . . in a good way.

"Why," the woman cried (only it came out *vhy*), "we have heard so many good things about you, Princess! You are a friend of our son, Prince Gunther. I am Princess Anna-Katerina Lapsburg von Stuben, and this is my husband, Prince Hans."

I nearly fainted right there on the top of the mountain. I was talking to Prince Gunther's parents, the Prince and Princess of Stockerdörfl! (Stockerdörfl is a principality, just like Genovia, which means it's ruled by a prince or princess, not a king or queen. Except that it's not, since the aristocracy was abolished in Austria many years ago.)

"Your Highnesses," I said, trying to curtsy in my ski boots and skis, which isn't easy, let me tell you. "It's so nice to meet you. Prince Gunther has said so many nice things about you, too. And I'm looking forward to having dinner at your home tonight."

"And we are looking forward to having you!"

Princess Anna-Katerina is the most beautiful lady I'd ever seen, with the exception of my sister and Beyoncé. She has curly blond hair and perfectly made-up lips and eyes, despite the fact that she'd been out all day, skiing. "Hans, shall we ski her down the mountain?"

"Yes, of course—with your permission, madame?"

I don't know if Serena particularly liked being called "madame"—back at the RGG barracks, her rank is lieutenant—but she nodded politely to indicate that the prince could help.

Prince Hans held his ski pole out in front of him. "Just hold on to this, Your Highness. We will take care of the rest."

I had no idea what he was talking about, but Serena seemed to catch on.

"Oh," she said. "Are you certain, Prince Hans? We wouldn't like to spoil your run."

"I have been skiing down this slope since I was a little boy," the prince said, sounding quite jolly—a bit like his son. "I can spend one run doing a good deed for another, especially given the fact that I own this mountain!"

So I did as the prince said, handing my ski poles off to Serena and awkwardly grabbing the middle of his ski pole, while he held one end, and his wife held the other. . . .

And the next thing I knew, I was skiing!

Really skiing, not beginner skiing like I'd been doing all day, but swooshing down the slope as fast as all the experienced skiers—as fast as Princess Komiko does her ski jumps.

Well, okay, maybe not that fast, but it seemed like it to me. Prince Hans and Princess Anna-Katerina were probably actually going pretty slow, guiding me down the mountain between them, but to a beginning skier like me, it seemed super fast . . . so fast that tears streamed down my face (because, like any amateur, I forgot to lower my goggles). The wind was so cold, and bits of snow and ice were flying up into my face from the prince's and princess's skis.

But I didn't care. I loved it! Because we were going *so fast*, and it was SO FUN!

Now I understood, even more than before, why people love winter sports so much. It isn't just about the snowball fights and fondue and sitting around the fire. It's about the thrill of gliding down a mountain as fast as you can go on a couple of tiny pieces of wood.

When the Lapsburg von Stubens slid to a graceful stop at the front of the Eis Schloss, I wasn't sure who was sadder—me, because my ride down the mountain was over, or Luisa since she was walking out of the hotel at the exact same time, with the Duke of Marborough at her side.

"Hi," I said, as casually as possible, wiping my lenses off on my neck warmer so I'd be sure to get a really good look at her. I wanted to see her expression. "Have you met Prince Hans and Princess Anna-Katerina yet, Lady Luisa? They're Prince Gunther's parents."

Luisa turned bright red.

"Oh, er," she stammered. "Your Highnesses. How

do you, er, do?" She fumbled a curtsy, looking as if she might pass dead away into the snow from shock.

I couldn't blame her, really. I would be embarrassed, too, if I suddenly bumped into my boyfriend's parents while I was with the Duke of Marborough, the boy I'd been kissing behind my boyfriend's back.

"Lady Luisa," Princess Anna-Katerina said, looking genuinely pleased. "How lovely to see you! You look even prettier than in the pictures Gunther's showed us." She leaned down to give my cousin a huge hug, then kissed her on both cheeks. "Welcome to Stockerdörfl!"

Luisa looked even more startled by the warmth of the welcome she was getting from her boyfriend's parents. "Oh," she said. "Um . . . thank you. Thank you so much."

"Such a pretty girl," Prince Hans said, shaking Luisa's hand. Well, more like shaking all of Luisa, because he was pumping her arm up and down with so much force. "Wouldn't you say, Anna-Katerina? And smart, too, from what Gunther tells us. You like school, Lady Luisa?"

"Um," Luisa said. "Yes. Yes, I do, Your Highness."

"Good," Prince Hans said. "Good, good! That is very good. It is good for Gunther to be with a girl who likes school. Because Gunther, he did not like school very much until this year, wouldn't you say, Anna-Katerina?"

"He liked it a bit toward the end of last year," Princess Anna-Katerina said. "When Princess Olivia invited him to her sister's wedding, which sadly we could not attend. But that's where he met a certain someone. I wonder who!" She smiled kindly at Luisa.

I wondered if the guilt was eating away at my cousin yet. She did look as if she felt really uncomfortable. The Duke of Marborough, standing behind her, had pulled out his cell phone and begun playing a game.

If my grandmother had caught me playing a game on my phone in front of my royal elders, she'd have done to me what she had to the duke and his Tupac shirt: whipped the cell phone out of my hands and given it to someone else—or stomped it to bits beneath her boots.

But fortunately for the duke, Grandmère wasn't there to witness this rude behavior.

Prince Gunther, Princess Komiko, Nadia, Prince Khalil, and the others were, though. They'd made it down the mountain and were removing their skis before heading off to the next event. Prince Gunther noticed Luisa first and was waving hello, when he spied his parents.

"Father!" Prince Gunther ran to his dad to hug him. Then he hugged his mother. "Come and meet my friends!"

Luisa, meanwhile, took the opportunity to grab me by the arm.

"How did you manage that, Stick?" she hissed.

"Manage what?" I whispered back.

"You know what I mean," Luisa said. "How did you manage to meet Prince Gunther's parents?"

"Oh," I said. "That. Well, for one thing, I didn't go sneaking off to lunch with the Twelfth Duke of Marborough."

She widened her eyes at me. "WHAT?"

"I think you heard me."

I was really mad at her, and skiing down the mountain—even with the assistance of the Prince and Princess of Stockerdörfl—had given me the confidence to finally confront her. "I saw you last night in the lobby, kissing the duke."

Luisa's face turned the same pink color as her skating dress, which she'd changed into for the figure skating competition, which started in one hour.

"I . . . that was only . . ."

"It's none of my business who you kiss," I whispered. "I really don't care. But Prince Gunther is my friend, and I thought he was yours, too. What you are doing to him is very rude. We are guests in his country right now, and so we should be especially courteous to him and his family, since they're hosting this event. If you don't have a crush on him anymore, that's fine, but you should have the maturity to tell him so, or at least not sneak around behind his back with some other boy. Otherwise, he's going to find out from someone else, and it's going to hurt his feelings."

Luisa seemed to recover a bit from her initial shock.

"Since when do *you* care so much about Prince Gunther's feelings?" she demanded, narrowing her eyes. "I thought you liked Prince Khalil."

Now it was my turn to blush. "I do," I said. "But only as a friend."

"Oh, right." Luisa let out an unpleasant laugh. "That's why you were hanging out with him so much this summer, and taking so many photos of him at the hockey game earlier."

She said this pretty loudly. Loudly enough that several people looked over at us, including Prince Khalil.

"I don't know what you're talking about," I whispered, feeling myself blush even more deeply. I hoped I was bundled up in enough layers against the cold that no one would notice. "Of course I was taking photos of him. That's my job! I'm the school photographer."

"Sure," Luisa said with a sneer. "Since when is it the school photographer's job to take photos of someone with his shirt off at the train station? Don't try to act like you didn't. *I saw you do it.*"

If there had been an avalanche right then and there—just a huge wall of snow, tumbling down the mountainside, to bury me alive—I would have been totally grateful. I could not believe she'd seen me take that photo of Prince Khalil. This was seriously the most embarrassing thing that had ever happened to me.

And I was pretty sure Prince Khalil had heard her say it.

"Listen, Luisa," I said, grabbing her arm and turning her around so that Prince Khalil—who was definitely looking in our direction—couldn't see our faces. "You're right, okay? I did take that photo. But I had to. I lost a bet with my friend Nishi."

"Oh, right!" Luisa laughed even more unpleasantly. "That photo is for your friend Nishi, and not because you have a total crush on Prince Khalil. I completely believe you, Olivia." Her voice dripped with sarcasm.

Now I was getting desperate. "Fine, Luisa. You

don't have to believe me, even though it's the honest truth." I took out my cell phone. "I can show you our text messages—"

"I don't care about your stupid text messages," Luisa said, snatching my phone away. "All I care about is the fact that you try to act so high-and-mighty and better than me when the truth is you're just as bad. You gamble, you take photos of boys behind their backs—or should I say, under their shirts—and you judge people when you have no right to." She began scrolling through the photos on my phone. "And I think it's about time that people learn the truth about their precious little Princess Olivia—"

My heart began to thump hard. Luisa was right. I didn't have any right to judge her. I really was just as bad as she was.

"Let's see," Luisa said, gazing down at my photos. "What do we have here? What photos do you think certain people we go to school with might find most interesting?"

"Luisa." I felt as if an unseen hand were

clutching my throat. "Please don't. Give me my phone back. You really shouldn't do this. Think of Genovia. We're both representing—"

"Uh-huh. Genovia." Luisa smirked, not even looking up from my phone screen. "You care a ton about *Genovia*."

It was right then that Rocky did something that forever made him my favorite person in the whole world.

He came running over and grabbed the edge of my jacket.

I don't think I'd ever been so glad to see anyone in my life.

"Olivia," he cried. "The dogsledding competition is starting! Are you coming? Because I'm in it! You have to come and take pictures!"

I looked down at him. I wanted to throw my arms around him and squeeze him. But instead I pretended to be mad. "What do you mean, you're in it? You better not be. I told you Snowball is not—"

"Not with Snowball," Rocky said scornfully.

"She's too spoiled to pull anything. The Prince of Bahrain has *real* sled dogs, and he's going to let me be the musher, since I'm so little. He says the sled will go super fast with me in it."

I glared at him. "Snowball is not spoiled. And mushing is dangerous! You don't have any experience."

And just like that, I reached over and snatched my phone from Luisa's hands.

"I better get over there," I said loudly, "and give the prince a piece of my mind."

"What?" Rocky cried. "No, you can't! Olivia, come *on*. Just this one time, let me have some fun!"

"Well," I said, glancing over my shoulder to see if Prince Khalil was watching . . . but fortunately, he was not. He'd turned his attention to the video game the Duke of Marborough was playing. He and Tots and the duke seemed to be discussing the finer points of the game.

Which was a relief. It meant he might not have overheard as much of my conversation with my cousin as I'd thought.

"Well," I said, turning back to Luisa. "Looks like I have to go now. I guess we'll have to continue this conversation later."

"Oh," Luisa said, tossing her long blond ponytail with enough force to make it bounce. "Don't worry. We *will* be continuing this conversation later."

Ugh.

Probably I should have just kept my mouth shut.

Thursday, November 26
6:00 P.M.
Eis Schloss

Everyone is changing for dinner at the Lapsburg von Stubens' house. I've never seen people so excited. Someone checked the address on Google Earth so we could see what the place looks like, and it turns out that Prince Gunther lives in a castle. . . .

Not a boring palace like mine, but an *actual castle*, with a moat and a drawbridge and towers and everything.

I'm pretty sure Google is wrong. Every time

Prince Gunther said he was going home, he said "to my *house*," not "to my *castle*."

But I'm keeping my opinions to myself, because:

A. The last time I opened my mouth, it got me in big trouble.
B. Today has been a very hard day for the athletes of the Royal Genovian Academy.

Not only did Rocky lose his dogsled race (no wonder: I don't know why anyone would let a ten-year-old who's never mushed before be a musher in a competition. The good thing is, he didn't get hurt—though his team did come in last—and he had a great time. He now says he wants to be a professional dogsled racer when he grows up. He's texted Dad asking him to please buy twelve Alaskan malamutes), but both Luisa and Nadia lost in the figure skating semifinals to a girl from TRAIS.

While I felt bad for Nadia, I can't say I felt too bad for Luisa, especially since she didn't even show good sportswomanship about it: She refused to go up and shake the hand of the first-place winner after the competition, even though she (and Nadia) did well enough to compete tomorrow in the finals!

Grandmère was appalled.

"There is nothing worse," she remarked as Luisa came out of the rink, "than a sore loser."

Luisa tossed her golden head. "What is the point of playing," she asked, "if you don't win?"

"The point is that you've spent time participating in an activity you've enjoyed, in the company of good friends." Grandmère lowered her sunglasses so that she could better pin Luisa with one of her most crushing looks. "You will find, as you get older, that that is the very definition of winning."

Luisa rolled her eyes and huffed away from us . . .

straight into the arms of Prince Gunther, who was waiting for her with a huge teddy bear he'd bought from a local gift shop! The teddy bear was holding a heart and a real red rose between its paws.

"For you!" Prince Gunther cried. "You will always be a winner to me, Lady Luisa!"

"Oh, Gunther," she muttered, looking around to see if anyone had noticed (which was silly, since *everyone* had noticed. Who isn't going to notice a boy standing there with a giant teddy bear?).

Luisa wasn't very nice about it, though. She snatched the bear out of his arms and crumpled it up against her stomach, so it would be less obvious. "You shouldn't have."

"Do you like it?" Prince Gunther asked. "I thought you would, because it is yellow, like my hair. I thought you could call it Goo Goo Bear, like you call me!"

Luisa looked like she wanted to die . . . especially when over to the side, the Duke of Marborough and the Marquis of Tottingham, who'd also been watching Luisa's performance, began to laugh.

"Goo Goo Bear!" the duke cried with a laugh. "That's awesome. Hey, Ferrari! Why don't you give your Goo Goo Bear a kiss?"

Luisa began blushing as red as the rose Goo Goo Bear was holding.

"Shut up, Marby," she snapped.

"Well." Prince Gunther, not having noticed the exchange, waved to us all. "Good-bye. I have to get to my event. Wish me luck!"

"Good luck, Goo Goo Bear!" called Tots, laughing . . . at least until my grandmother stood up and gave him and the duke her most evil stare. Then they suddenly found nothing funny at all about the situation, and quickly left the skating arena.

This dinner is going to be a disaster . . . not just because I'm pretty sure Prince Khalil overheard Luisa saying that I have a crush on him, but because Grandmère just told me I have to give a speech.

"Stockerdörfl has the second highest number of tourists this time of year of any area in Europe," Grandmère said, when I stopped by her penthouse suite (which is so huge, it makes the large room I'm sharing with Nadia and Princess Komiko look like a playpen) to make sure she approved of my outfit for the evening. Francesca had picked it out—a demure black velvet dress—so of course Grandmère approved. "Second highest in a *normal* year, that is. Do you know who is first, Olivia?"

I wasn't sure, but I could guess. "Disney World, in Orlando?"

"Of course not! Genovia. But this year, because the media has declared that Genovia is some kind of toxic zone due to La Grippe, which we both know to be a tiny little cold—hardly worth mentioning, except to a hysteric like your sister—Stockerdörfl is now the number one tourist destination in Europe. You need to put an end to that tonight by inviting the Lapsburg von Stubens to visit us in Genovia, and getting them to agree to come, hopefully sometime soon. If they're photographed on one of our beaches—they're very popular with the media, you know, because they're both so young and rich and attractive and sporty—it could really turn things around. If the Lapsburg von Stubens aren't afraid of catching La Grippe, the rest of Europe's jet set won't be."

I held out my hands in a helpless gesture. "I mean . . . sure, Grandmère. I can try. But isn't that kind of using them?"

"Of course, it is, Olivia! But don't think they aren't using your visit here to promote their winter sports venues. That is how celebrity works. Now, will you do it, or not?"

"Sure, Grandmère," I said. "Geesh. You don't have to yell."

"I'm not yelling, Olivia. I'm merely suffering from a bit of indigestion from lunch. I ran into my old friend the Swedish ambassador, and I might have overimbibed a bit."

"Oh. I'm sorry, Grandmère."

I didn't say anything more—like how it would be nice if someone would tell me these things more than five minutes beforehand, so I'd have time to practice.

But that would be asking my family to be normal, which is like asking it not to snow in Stockerdörfl in the wintertime.

And now I'm back in the hotel room, and I don't even feel that badly for Nadia anymore for losing in the skating semifinals, because of what is sitting on her bed.

"What's *he* doing in here?" I demanded.

Nadia shrugged while putting on her lip gloss in the bathroom mirror. "Luisa was throwing him out. So now he's mine."

"Luisa was *throwing him out*?" I couldn't believe it. "In the trash?"

"Yes," Nadia said. "I saw the maid taking him away in her cart. So I knocked on Luisa and Victorine's door and asked Luisa if I could have him, and she said if I wanted to be an immature baby who collects stuffed animals, I should be her guest. So now I am an immature baby with a cute teddy bear, I guess!"

Ugh! I couldn't believe my cousin sometimes. "Well, don't let Prince Gunther see that you have Goo Goo Bear, okay?"

Nadia looked at my reflection in the bathroom mirror. "Of course not! That would break his heart."

I sighed.

Honestly, sometimes the royals around here are the ones who act like they've had no etiquette training whatsoever.

Which I guess according to Luisa includes me.

But I sent Nishi all the photos of Prince Khalil that she asked for, and told her that my end of the debt is fulfilled. Then I deleted them from my phone.

So now there is no longer any evidence that I behaved in a nonroyal manner.

Or at least there better not be.

Friday, November 27
1:00 A.M.
Eis Schloss

Okay, so Prince Gunther *does* live in a castle!

It really is a true, honest-to-goodness medieval castle, built into the side of a mountain, with a moat around it (well, the part that's not built into the mountain, anyway).

That's why it's called Wasser Schloss. *Wasser* means water.

Only, in winter the water freezes and makes these beautiful ice sculptures, and Prince Gunther's parents shine these different-colored lights on them.

So as we were coming up the side of the mountain on the bus, it looked like we were approaching Elsa's castle from the movie *Frozen*.

Everyone started *ooh*ing and *aah*ing and getting out their cell phones so that they could take photos of it, then posting the photos to their social media accounts.

I totally would not have been surprised if a talking snowman and a deer with giant antlers had run out to greet us as we were getting off the bus.

But instead, we were greeted by Prince Hans and Princess Anna-Katerina Lapsburg von Stuben, looking even more glamorous than when I'd seen them on the ski slope . . . because now they were dressed in evening wear!

Prince Hans had on a tuxedo, and Princess Anna-Katerina was wearing a white gown that sparkled more than the icicles hanging off the gargoyles on her castle (which were kind of creepy-looking. I was glad there were such cheerful colored lights pointing up at them, because in different circumstances, you might definitely think of it as Dracula's castle. Also if it was in Romania and not Austria).

"Good evening, children," Prince Hans said in a hearty, welcoming voice. "We are so glad you could make it tonight to our humble home!"

Humble? It had to have thirty bedrooms, at least. There was a drawbridge! And that's not to mention the torches—lit with *real fire*—that danced everywhere outside.

"We hope your journey has not caused you to become too cold, but in case it has, we have prepared some hot cider to warm you."

From behind the prince came cheerful uniformed servants, all bearing trays of steaming silver cups.

"Please," Prince Hans said, taking a cup from one of the trays and raising it toward us. "Come in!"

"Very gracious," Grandmère said—because of course all the chaperones had been invited, too, though none of the bodyguards, since Prince Hans had his own security, and it was presumed we'd all be safe in his castle, which had been built with the idea to protect its inhabitants from assaults from all sides. She took a cup from one of the trays and raised it toward our host and hostess. "The princes of Stockerdörfl have always been skilled at entertaining, however. Prince Hans's father—God rest his soul—used to have the best ski parties in Europe."

"This cider is good," I said. It really was. "And this castle is amazing!"

There was a large roaring fire as soon as you walked in that instantly warmed you, as well as a chandelier hanging overhead that appeared to be made out of pure solid . . .

"Is that *gold*?" Luisa cried, her face turned upward.

"Ah, indeed it is," Prince Hans said, smiling at her. "Many centuries ago, before these mountains became known for their amazing skiing, they held immense stores of gold. My ancestors were the first to mine them."

Luisa couldn't tear her gaze from the Great Hall's ceiling, which in addition to having a beautiful gold chandelier also bore a brightly colored mural of angels and cherubim flitting across a blue—and gold—sky.

I wondered what Luisa was thinking. Probably that she should have kept Goo Goo Bear, because the boy who had given it to her was way richer than she'd thought.

"Father," Prince Gunther said, "shall I show them the rest of the house?"

House! Ha!

"Yes, son," Prince Hans said. "Go right ahead. But dinner will be served soon in the East Dining Room, so come right back."

"Of course, Father."

Prince Gunther showed us—kids, not adults; the adults went with the Prince and Princess of Stockerdörfl into the library to enjoy cocktails—all around the castle, including the billiard room and ballroom, the media room, the stables and the pool, the dungeons and the towers, and of course his room, on the walls of which hung many photos of his Olympic swimming heroes.

The boys—and a lot of the girls, too—really liked Prince Gunther's room, because he had every video game ever invented, practically.

But we didn't get to linger long in there, because soon a gong rang, indicating that dinner was ready.

The East Dining Room was almost bigger than the ballroom in the palace back in Genovia! It too had an enormous gold chandelier, and tapestries hanging from the wood rafters in the ceiling depicted dancing ladies and knights battling a terrible dragon. The table was so long, they'd had to set it with place cards (just like lunch back at school!) so that everyone could find his or her seat.

I was relieved that I hadn't been seated near Rocky or Grandmère. She'd been put near the head of the table, by Prince Hans, because it's traditional at formal dinner parties for the eldest, highest-ranked lady to be placed near the host.

But while I was happy to find that I was seated at the other end of the table, next to beautiful Princess Anna-Katerina, I was not so happy to discover that I also had to sit beside my cousin Luisa.

Ugh!

But there is nothing ruder than asking a hostess to move your seat assignment (well, there are lots of ruder things, actually. Grabbing fistfuls of your food, yelling, "I hate this!" and throwing it at the walls would be ruder. But I would never do that).

So instead of asking to be moved, I said simply, "Oh, the flowers on your table are so lovely, Your Highness. Thank you so much for having us," to Princess Anna-Katerina, and sat down and put my napkin in my lap.

"Thank *you* so much, Princess Olivia, for coming," Prince Gunther's mother said, smiling back at me. "I've always been so fond of roses. Though they are, of course, terribly hard to find this time of year."

"Not in Genovia," I said. Wow, this was almost too easy! Now I could issue the invitation Grandmère had asked me to give Prince Gunther's parents, and it would seem totally natural. "We have them year round. We have them blooming in the Royal Genovian Gardens right now. You're welcome to come visit anytime and see. Maybe next weekend, if you and your husband would like to?"

Princess Anna-Katerina looked surprised.

"Oh, Your Highness," she said. "What a lovely invitation!"

"Yes, Mother," Prince Gunther said. He was seated across from me. "Say you'll come! You have to! Next weekend is the Genovian Lobster Festival. It will be so jolly!"

Princess Anna-Katerina smiled. "It's lovely to see Gunther as excited about something as he is about Genovia, Princess Olivia," she said, with a sparkle in her eye. "Of course Hans and I will come to visit. We would be delighted to. But are you sure your family will want visitors so soon? Your sister has just had twins, I understand."

"Oh," I said. "I'm sure. We don't have as many guest rooms as you do, but we have quite a few."

"Well," Princess Anna-Katerina said. "Then we would be delighted. I do love babies so."

"*Wunderbar!*" Prince Gunther cried.

He wasn't the only one who was happy. I'd done what Grandmère had asked me to! I'd invited Prince Gunther's parents to Genovia . . . and they'd said yes!

After that, I felt like I had made up for some of the terrible things I'd done—sneaking that photo of Prince Khalil with no shirt on, and being so judgmental of Luisa.

Now maybe I could relax a little, and have fun.

I should have known better, of course. Because as soon as dinner was over Prince Hans stood up and suggested we all step out onto the terrace for a moment with our Apfelstrudel (which is Austrian apple strudel). He had something he wanted to show us.

The something turned out to be fireworks!

They weren't as spectacular as the fireworks we have in Genovia, of course, because if they set off really big fireworks in the Alps, the explosive percussion could cause an avalanche.

But it was a nice low-key fireworks show (done with approval of the Stockerdörfl ski patrol. They set off small explosions every day to cause unstable snowpacks to slide off in a controlled manner and reduce the risk of skiers being injured in unplanned avalanches).

It was really cold out on the terrace, and none of us had our coats on because we'd given them to the footmen. So while we stood watching the show, some of us clustered together for warmth. I clustered together with Princess Komiko, Nadia, and Victorine, who was hugging Rocky (he's so snuggly when he wants to be. Other times he will fart on you and laugh).

Luisa clustered with Prince Gunther. He put his jacket around her and hugged her.

It was disgusting.

I tried not to notice that Prince Khalil was standing by himself only a few feet away from me, his hands in the pockets of his suit trousers. He didn't once look my way during the fireworks, unlike the Duke of Marborough, who stared at Lady Luisa Ferrari the entire time.

All Prince Khalil looked was sad.

I couldn't help wondering if visiting Prince Gunther's house had reminded him of nice times he used to have with his family back in Qalif, a place he'll probably never be able to return to again. Wondering that made me feel a little sad, too, and homesick for Genovia.

After the fireworks show, it was time to leave. Remembering my manners, I curtsied to Gunther's parents and thanked them for the meal, mentioning again how much we'd enjoy seeing them in Genovia.

They told *me* again how nice it had been to meet me, and asked me to come back and visit them in Stockerdörfl anytime I wanted.

"What was *that* all about?" Luisa asked sourly as I climbed onto the bus.

"What was what all about?"

"That little meeting you and Gunther's parents had back there."

"Oh," I said. "Nothing. I just said thank you, and they invited me to come visit them again sometime."

"They didn't invite *me* to come visit them again sometime," Luisa said grumpily.

"You're not the princess of the country whose school their son goes to," Victorine reminded her.

"Hmph," Luisa said, and looked around the crowded bus for the duke.

But before she had a chance to find him, Jasmine, the coolest senior girl in our school now that Queen Amina had graduated and gone back to her country to rule, waved to her and said, "Luisa! Here's a spot. You can sit here."

Luisa, looking startled—she'd been scanning the bus for a certain person, not a seat—gave Jasmine a smile. "Um, thank you so much, but I don't really—"

"No, take it," Jasmine said. "It's fine!"

"Um, thanks," Luisa said, and slid into the available seat. "Uh . . . Jasmine, is it?"

Jasmine is the goalie on our school's girls' hockey team, so for Luisa to have pretended not to know her name was pretty insulting. She'd only done so because Jasmine isn't royal.

Jasmine is very patient and kind, however. She said, "Yes. Will I see you at the finals tomorrow?"

"I'll be there," I said, even though no one had asked me. I often find that inserting myself into other people's conversations is a good way to help with diplomatic relations. I held up my phone. "I'm taking photos for the school paper and yearbook. I hope you kick FARs' butts! Especially that goalie of theirs."

Jasmine laughed and raised her knuckles to fist-bump me. I fist-bumped her back . . . just as Prince Khalil walked by to find a seat on the bus.

I'm pretty sure he overheard me tell the star goalie of our girls' hockey team to kick the butt of the girl Victorine says he liked last year.

So much for diplomatic relations.

Oh well. Even though I'm a princess, I'm not good at *everything*. Yet.

Friday, November 27
7:00 A.M.
Eis Schloss

Something weird just happened. I mean, even weirder than usual.

Nadia and Princess Komiko and I were having breakfast in the hotel when Prince Gunther came up to our table, carrying a steaming mug of coffee.

"Hi, Prince Gunther," I said. "Do you want to sit with us?"

We scooted our stuff over to make room for him, but it turned out he didn't want to sit with us. He wanted to talk. To me.

Alone.

I swallowed and threw the girls a panicky look behind the prince's back. "Um, sure, Prince Gunther."

I got up and followed him to a nearby table. It was beside one of the enormous picture windows looking out across the mountains, snowcapped and majestic against a sky that was already promising to be as clear blue as yesterday's.

"I really do love your village," I said as I sat down, since I got the feeling he could use some cheering up. He hadn't smiled once since coming into the dining room. "It's just so charming. And the people are so kind. And I so enjoyed meeting your parents last night. They are the nicest people."

I was aware that I was babbling, but that's what you do when the boy your cousin is cheating on asks if he can talk to you alone at breakfast.

"Thanks," he said. "Pastry?"

"Sure," I said, and took one to be polite. "So what's the matter?"

I already knew what the matter was, though. So when he said it, I wasn't surprised.

"Luisa." He exhaled, and a plume of flaky crumbs flew out of his mouth and landed in a gentle fan pattern across the table. "Have you seen how she is acting? What am I saying, of course you have, she is your cousin. Olivia, I am sorry to put you in the middle, but I do not know who else to turn to. There are times—like yesterday, at the skating event, with Goo Goo Bear—when I think she does not even like me. That maybe . . . this is hard for me to say, but sometimes I think that she likes someone else. And the truth is . . . well, there are times when I think I like someone else, too."

"Gunther!" I cried, reaching out and grasping his hand. "I'm so sorry! But if you like someone else, that would be *amazing*! I mean—"

Seeing the look on his face—a mix of wonder and alarm—I quickly let go of his hand.

"I mean, that's so interesting. If you like someone else, and you think Luisa likes someone else, maybe it's time for you two to stop being boyfriend and girlfriend, and just be friends. Then no one will get hurt. Right?"

He looked down at his wrist. "But . . . what about this?"

I remembered the bracelets Luisa had gotten them that said *L + G*.

"Oh. Well, you'll have to give yours back. I think that's the polite thing to do."

He considered this. "And what about our matching evening wear?" he asked. It came out *ewening vear*. "We are both wearing Claudio to your birthday ball tomorrow night."

"Oh, Gunther," I said. "That's all right. You can still wear matching clothes and just be friends."

He thought about this. "Well, yes . . . I guess so."

"Look," I said. "You don't have to do anything right now. Why don't you talk to her first, and see how it goes. Maybe everything will work out."

I knew everything wasn't going to work out, but people could still surprise you.

Prince Gunther smiled for the first time since he'd sat down.

"All right," he said. "Thank you, Princess Olivia, for this advice. I knew if I came to you, you would help me. You are the person who has always been nicest to me in the whole world . . . except for my parents, of course."

"Aw," I said, and patted him on the hand. "Thank you, Gunther. I'm glad we're friends."

"I'm glad, too," he said. "My parents are also glad. They told me last night that they think you are the nicest, most polite girl."

This was good to hear. Who doesn't like hearing that someone thinks they're nice?

"I liked them, too," I said. "Are they going to watch you ski today?"

"Snowboard, and yes. Then they will hand out the medals at the closing ceremony."

"That's right!" I said. "I forgot. Then I can see them before we leave."

"Oh," Prince Gunther said, his smile growing broader. "You will see them for sure before you leave."

"Great," I said, and got up to go back to my own table. "I'm glad we had this little talk."

"I am, too," said Prince Gunther, and waved at me, and at Snowball as well, because of course she was with me. She goes everywhere with me (that dogs are allowed).

I felt much better about things after that.

At least until Grandmère signaled to me from where she was sitting in the dining room and waved for me to come over.

"What was that all about?" she wanted to know.

No "Good morning, Olivia" or "How did you sleep, Olivia?" Just "What was that all about?"

But that's how my grandmother is. She likes to get straight to the point, especially early in the morning, before she's had her coffee, and of course her hot water with lemon.

"Well," I said, "I think Prince Gunther is going to break up with Luisa."

"Is he?" Grandmère asked, taking a sip of her coffee. "Because of the Duke of Marborough, I suppose."

I was surprised. "You *know* about that?"

"I'm a chaperone, Olivia. Of course I know about that."

"Oh." I thought about this. "Well, I was worried about his feelings getting hurt, but he says he likes someone else."

"Does he, now?" Grandmère sipped her hot water with lemon. "And who might that be?"

"I don't know," I said. "I hope it's Nadia. I think she likes him. She took the teddy bear he gave Luisa out of the trash and kept it."

"Hmmm," Grandmère said. "Well, let's hope you are right, and that the young lady's affections are returned. Run along now, or you will be late."

I looked at the time on her diamond watch. "You're right! See you later, Grandmère!"

Friday, November 27
1:00 P.M.
Eis Schloss

< NishiGirl

Thanks for the photos, Olivia, but I cannot even see Prince Khalil's face in most of them because he's wearing a hockey helmet.

And what are these photos of him fighting? Why did he get into a fight? I didn't think princes got into fights (except over a girl's honor). Dylan, the boy in my English class, would never get into a fight. He has the soul of a poet.

The photo of Prince Khalil with his shirt off is pretty good, but you can't see his face because it's inside the shirt! It could be any boy.

I'm not sure these photos count toward our bet. I'll have to think about it.
I still love you, though. XOXOX

Ugggh. Nishi is going to drive me insane.

Friday, November 27
5:00 P.M.
Train Back to Genovia

We won!!!!

It was really close, but the girls from the RGA hockey team (plus Prince Gunther and the other snowboarders) pulled it off.

The RGA boys' hockey team lost. Actually, they didn't just lose. They didn't even play. They were disqualified due to unsportsmanlike behavior for fighting (!) before the game even started. I am sorry to have to write those words, but they're true. Grandmère is extremely disappointed in them.

Grandmère is extremely disappointed in a lot of people (and things), but thankfully I am not one of them.

When the fight broke out, I maintained my composure, and kept on taking pictures like a professional photographer is supposed to do (even if Nishi doesn't like my photos).

But I also ran to the nearest responsible person and told them to call an ambulance.

Fortunately the ambulance was not needed because no one was seriously hurt, although the 12th Duke of Marborough does have a black eye. I think this is only fair, since he is the one who started the fight.

It was during the introductions, when the players from each team were announced. As the duke's name was announced and he glided out onto the ice, someone on The Royal Academy in Switzerland team shouted, "Genovian Fondue-Fork Licker!"

I've never heard that it's a breach in etiquette to lick your fondue fork (though Grandmère says you should never, ever lick your knife), and being called a Genovian . . . well, that's a compliment.

But not to the duke, apparently, who skated over and punched the person who called him a Genovian Fondue-Fork Licker in the face.

I've been punched in the face before, and let me tell you: it hurts.

Resorting to violence is never the answer, but . . . well, I didn't really blame the duke for punching that guy. No one wants to be called a Fondue-Fork Licker.

And the duke isn't even Genovian! He's 100 percent British.

The duke punching the guy (who turned out to be a Saudi prince—oops) caused all the other members of The Royal Academy in Switzerland boys' hockey team to jump up to defend their teammate, and all the members of the Royal Genovian Academy's boys' hockey team to rush out onto the ice to do the same.

It was complete chaos.

"What was I supposed to do?" the duke demanded later. "I couldn't let them get away with calling me a fork licker."

"Actually," Grandmère said, "you should have. Because by refusing to ignore something so idiotic, you've let down all your teammates, as well as your school. It is lucky for you that your fellow classmates are more mature, because that is the only way we've won today—though it's a hollow victory."

Grandmère said all this into the microphone during the medals ceremony, when she was supposed to be talking about the history of the Royal School Winter Games.

Instead she talked about how she considers our victory today hollow because they canceled the biathlon. This was due to the controversial issue of allowing young royals to have access to guns. Should young royals have access to guns? Grandmère's opinion is yes, for sports, with supervision.

"In my day—"

Madame Alain stepped up to the podium and tried to take the microphone from Grandmère's hand.

"So sorry, Your Highness," she said. "But we need to move along. We only have the room until three."

But Grandmère clung tightly to both the microphone and the podium.

"This generation of royals is going to grow up weak and spoiled, with no idea how to defend themselves when confronted by an enemy!" she cried as they dragged her off.

Though later Prince Hans jokingly reminded her, as he handed out the medals for best sportsmanship, that the 12th Duke of Marborough seemed to have proven that shouldn't be a problem.

A lot of people—like Prince Khalil—are so mad at the duke that they are not even speaking to him. Prince Khalil is sitting with us (!!!!) here on the train, having a very nice time enjoying the picnic basket that Prince Hans and Princess Anna-Katerina prepared for our victory trip home.

I only wish everyone could be as happy as we are (well, I'm not COMPLETELY happy. Prince Khalil has been on his cell phone for a large part of the trip. I don't know who he is texting, but I suspect it might be Princess Sophie. I am very sorry that her team was defeated by ours, but does she really need to spend THAT much time texting about her humiliating loss with a boy who goes to the school that crushed hers? That is simply sad, if you ask me).

The person I really mean is Prince Gunther. He is very unhappy, because after the fight was over, everyone saw how Luisa ran over to the duke and held a snowball to his eye to try to help him keep the swelling down and called him her "poor brave darling." Even Grandmère saw it, and told Luisa to stop being so foolish and let the ski patrol handle the duke's wounds.

I think Prince Gunther would have broken up with her then and there if he hadn't had to go to his snowboarding event.

But after Prince Gunther placed first in the boys' snowboard freestyle, and Luisa ran up to him and flung her arms around his neck and kissed him on the cheek and called him her "sweet Goo Goo Bear" (IN FRONT OF HIS PARENTS), we all saw the way he untangled himself from her and said, "Luisa, we need to talk."

!!!!!

I didn't get to see what happened next because Prince Gunther took Luisa by the arm and began walking her away (and Snowball started tugging on her leash, a sure sign she needed to take a pee).

Also, it's considered unroyal to eavesdrop on someone else's intimate conversation.

But the next time I saw the two of them, Prince Gunther was looking very grave, and Luisa had tears (real ones for once) running down her face.

"Is it for real this time?" Nadia whispered as we sat at the medals ceremony. Prince Gunther and Luisa were sitting several chairs apart. "Can they really be broken up?"

"Oh, it's real," Victorine whispered back. "I heard he gave her back his bracelet!"

"No way!" Princess Komiko looked shocked. "I never thought *he'd* break up with *her.*"

Truthfully, I never had either . . . even though I'd sort of advised him to.

Do I feel guilty about it? No.

Because right now Lady Luisa is sitting in the back of our train car, sharing earbuds and a music player with the Duke of Marborough, their heads bouncing in time to the beat. She doesn't look a bit sad . . . which is fine, I guess, since it's her life.

But you think she'd feel a *little* bit sad, since they went out for a long time . . . almost six months!

And Nadia, Princess Komiko, and Victorine are fighting (in a friendly way) over who gets to cheer up Prince Gunther. Right now, they're taking turns with Princess Komiko's fingernail polish, doing his nails, a different color for each hand. They say they're going to give him a pedicure next, if Grandmère doesn't yell at them for stinking up the train car and "acting like feather-headed fools."

Nadia has done a good job of hiding Goo Goo Bear in her luggage so Prince Gunther can't see that she has him. Even though Prince Gunther and Luisa are broken up now, we all thought it might be a bit too soon for the prince to see that Luisa abandoned it.

I'm doing pretty well, too, I guess. Well, except for Prince Khalil, who is still sitting next to me, texting with another woman (I know it's with a woman because I saw heart emojis).

Whatever. If Prince Khalil has decided to get back together with Princess Sophie, then I am happy for him. He's had a lot of heartache in his life lately, so he deserves to have some joy. I'm sure she's highly intelligent, an excellent hockey player (except for the time she was beaten by our immensely superior team), and extremely kind, as well.

So good for them. Who even cares about her, *or* Prince Khalil? There are way more important things to think about, such as:

Tomorrow is my birthday!!!

I already have an early birthday present in my pocket—Prince Gunther's parents gave it to me after they were done with the medals ceremony, as we were all saying good-bye and getting on the buses to go to the train station.

"You didn't have to do that!" I told them when Princess Anna-Katerina handed me the small gold-wrapped (of course) gift.

"Oh, we wanted to," she said. "You have been so kind to our son."

"Mother!" Prince Gunther cried, looking embarrassed.

Prince Hans laughed. "But you must promise not to open it until your birthday."

"Okay," I said. "I promise. Thank you very much."

I can't tell what's in the box, except that it's very heavy and clinks a little when I shake it. It's the right weight and size to be a key to the village of Stockerdörfl. That's something that people often give to visiting dignitaries—a key to their city.

It will be my first key ever!

I should start collecting them. Keys from cities all over the world.

That's pretty good, to get your first key to a city at thirteen. By the time I'm Grandmère's age, I should have a million.

Friday, November 27
10:30 P.M.
Royal Genovian Bedroom

Everything is so weird. My hands are shaking a little as I write this.

Not weird in a bad way, I think. Weird in a good way. Definitely a good way.

At least some of it. Not all, though. Definitely not all.

Everything was good at first. Every*one* is good. Better than good. Dr. Khan was here, checking on the babies.

She says Rocky and I are both completely healthy,

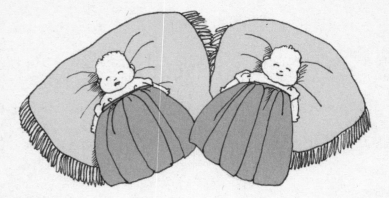

and the danger of either one of us passing a viral infection on to our niece and nephew is "negligible."

I could have told her that! Rocky and I are both very diligent about washing our hands before and after meals, and after using the restroom. (Well, I am. Rocky needs to be reminded, but that's what big sisters are for.)

Even better, the babies' heads are finally normal. They actually look cute now. I can't believe how much they've changed in just a few days!

Rocky took one look at them in their matching little cribs and blurted, "Aw, they're normal babies now, all cute and stuff."

Mia and Michael glanced at each other, confused. "What do you mean by 'normal,' Rocky?" she asked.

"Oh, nothing," I said quickly, covering for him. "Just that, um, they've lost that newborn glow."

I didn't have the heart to tell her the truth, that Rocky meant they no longer had pointy heads and were as red as newly cooked lobsters.

Mia looked down at the babies and said, "I think they still glow. You're glowing, aren't you, Elizabeth?"

"Elizabeth?" I echoed. "Who's Elizabeth?"

"Oh, did we forget to tell you?" Mia held up her baby daughter. "It hasn't been announced officially yet, but we're calling her Elizabeth after your mom, Olivia, whom we sadly never got to meet before she passed away. But from what I understand, she was a very strong, beautiful, and intelligent woman, and we're hoping our calling her Elizabeth will cause her to grow up to be just like her . . . and you, Olivia."

When I heard that—and saw the smile that my sister gave me over the warm pink bundle she was holding in her arms—tears of happiness filled my eyes.

But Mia wasn't finished.

"And we're calling our little boy Frank, after your dad, Rocky."

Rocky looked startled to hear this . . . so startled that he jerked his hands from the pockets of his trousers, causing a slingshot, two marbles, a Nintendo, and a dog biscuit to fall to the floor (Snowball immediately licked up the dog biscuit).

"You *are*?" Rocky's eyes were huge.

"Yes, we are," Mia said, too polite to mention all the detritus that had fallen onto the nursery floor from Rocky's pockets. "Because Frank Gianini was one of the smartest, nicest men I ever knew. I wish more than anything that he was still here with us. But since he too has passed away, at least he'll be here in name."

Rocky studied the face of his dad's namesake—Michael had taken Prince Frank from his crib—and said finally, "Good. Frank's a *much* better name than Star Fighter." Then he turned around and left the room, a definite spring in his step.

Mia and Michael looked at each other, more confused than ever.

I had to agree with Rocky, though. The names Elizabeth and Frank suited the new princess and prince of Genovia perfectly. The bookies in Las Vegas had been right all along.

But that's *still* not the weirdest thing that has happened. Not by a long shot.

Because later, Mia handed me the letter she'd texted me about . . . the one from my aunt in Qalif.

We weren't in the nursery anymore, but in the billiard room, where Lilly, who is Michael's sister—and who'd flown straight from New York City as soon as she'd heard her niece and nephew had been born—was hanging out with a newly opened bottle of Genovian wine.

"Wait a minute," I said, turning the envelope over. "This has been opened."

"Er," Mia said. "Well, yes. Due to security precautions, the Royal Genovian Press Office opens all our mail. They have to make sure that there isn't anything dangerous inside."

"What could my aunt have put inside a birthday card to me that's dangerous?" I asked.

"We were all thinking it would be laced with—"

Lilly began, but closed her mouth when Mia gave her a warning look.

"Nothing," Mia said quickly. "And it turns out that it isn't from your aunt at all."

"And it ain't no birthday card, either, kid," Lilly said, taking a sip from her wine. "But I got a feeling you're gonna like it anyway!"

"Lilly," Mia said.

"What?" Lilly shrugged. "She is!"

I shot them both a confused look, then opened the (already torn) envelope.

Inside was a letter written in cursive that I thought I recognized on royal stationery from the Throne of Qalif (which explained why it had been sent via royal post. All mail sent from countries with royal households arrives to the palace via special courier).

Sunday, November 22

Dear Princess Olivia,
Sorry if it seems weird that I'm writing

this to you. I promise I'm not weird. Well, maybe I'm a little weird, as you know. But that's something we both take pride in, right? ☺ ☺ ☺

But I'm afraid if I don't write this, there might never be a time when I can say what it is I want to say, between school, your busy royal schedule, my hockey games, and everything going on with my country (which as you know is really bad).

We haven't been getting to see each other as much as we used to, and that makes me sad, because I used to have so much fun coming over to your place, swimming, playing table tennis, and talking about iguanas and wildlife illustration.

You're the coolest girl I've ever met, and I just wanted to make sure you know that. I know it's been hard for you, moving to Genovia from America and having to get to know all new customs and even a new family. But I think you're doing a great job.

I'm really looking forward to hanging out with you at your birthday ball, and hopefully also at the Royal School Winter Games, if you come (I'm not sure if you're coming. I really, really hope you will).

I hope sometime when we both aren't so busy, we could go out for an ice cream or a coffee after school (if your father says it's all right). Because I really le like you, and I would like us to be better friends.

~~Love Your Friend~~ Sincerely,

Prince Khalil Rashid bin Zayed Faisal

P.S. I wrote this as a letter instead of a text because I always see you writing in your notebook, so I thought you'd like a letter better. I hope you don't think that's weird.

When I was done reading, I looked up and simply stared at Mia, too stunned to say a word.

"*Well?*" she said, her eyes bright with excitement. "What do you think?"

"It's the best letter you ever got," Lilly said. "Come on. Admit it. That's the best letter anyone ever got in their whole entire lives. Go ahead. You can say it."

But I didn't say that. Instead, I wailed, "But it's too late!"

"What do you mean, it's too late?" Mia asked. "Too late for what?"

"Yeah, really," Lilly said, taking another sip of her wine. "What are you, betrothed to someone else? You can't be. I do all the legal work around here, and I never saw a betrothal contract."

"No," I said. "It's not that."

I thought of the way Prince Khalil had told me I was "the opposite of a dork" Monday in the language lab at school, and how I'd "see." I hadn't understood what he'd been talking about then, but I got it now.

His letter! He'd been referring to his letter, and how I'd see what he meant—that he thought I was cool, and I'd know it when I got the letter he'd sent me, explaining his true feelings for me!

Only I hadn't responded. Not the next day. Not when he'd sat down next to me at fondue night. Not when he'd said I'd looked cute after the snowball fight. And even today, on the train, when he'd sat there beside me, texting, for hours!

I'd never mentioned a word about his letter or whether or not I wanted to go for ice cream (or a coffee). He must think I'm the rudest, snobbiest girl in the whole world!

"It's too late!" I cried again, sinking to the floor as if an avalanche back in Stockerdörfl had struck me dead (wishful thinking).

"How is it *too late*?" Mia cried. She sounded genuinely alarmed. I don't fling myself to the floor too often. Unlike my friends (and Mia) I'm not usually overdramatic about stuff.

I stared at the ceiling. "You say this came a few days ago?"

"Yes," Mia said, nodding. "Before you left. But it got lost in all the excitement with the babies and everything. I guess that's going to be a problem, going forward, with the three of you having birthdays so close together. But we'll tell the press office to be extra diligent. It will *never* happen again."

"Right," I said, sitting up. It was important to at least give the appearance of bravery, like all my Genovian ancestresses. "But Prince Khalil must have assumed I got it Monday night. I'm sure he's been waiting for me to say something about it *all week*. But I never did. So," I said with a sigh, "he got back together with his old girlfriend because he got tired of waiting around for me."

"WHAT?" Mia cried.

"How do you know that?" Lilly asked. As a corporate lawyer, she is very analytical. Plus, she loves to argue about everything, which was why her brother, Michael, hadn't joined us in the billiard room but had chosen to stay upstairs with the babies.

"Because he was texting her the whole train ride home," I explained, "even though he was sitting next to me. She sent him heart emojis. I didn't mean to spy, but I saw them."

Going over in my head every conversation Prince Khalil and I had had in the past week, it became more and more obvious. How cold and strange I must have seemed to him, never having mentioned his letter, or any part of what he'd said in it about liking me in any way!

It's true that he probably already thinks I'm weird—he mentioned this in his letter.

But now he must think me the biggest freak in the universe. What kind of girl gets asked out by a boy (via handwritten letter) and completely ignores it?

A weird girl. *The weirdest girl in the world.*

"Well," Mia said, "texting another girl doesn't mean he's back together with her. It could just mean he was . . . helping her with her homework. And she was grateful. So she sent him heart emojis to say thank you."

Even Lilly threw my sister an incredulous look.

"There was no homework this week. It was the Royal School Winter Games." I love my sister, but sometimes I think she doesn't know anything. "Oh,

God," I wailed, burying my face in my hands. "He must think I'm such a snob!"

"He doesn't think you're a snob," my sister said in a kind voice, gently patting my head. "It's a little misunderstanding. You could text him right now and tell him what happened—"

"*Text him?*"

I raised my head. Grandmère had walked into the room. Or rather . . . she'd swooped, as usual.

She had changed from her train clothes—a Chanel suit, fur coat, and heels—into her dressing gown and slippers. This time instead of a turban, there was night cream all over her face, except for two large spaces around her eyes.

But since this is how she dresses for bed every night, I wasn't scared . . . until I saw that she had Prince Khalil's letter in her hand and was reading it.

"You most certainly will NOT text him," Grandmère said. She'd found the letter lying on top of the Ping-Pong table and read it through the gold-rimmed lorgnettes she keeps in the pocket of her robe for this purpose. "When a man declares his affection for a woman in a handwritten love letter—sent by royal courier, no less—she does NOT respond to him by text. To do so would be crass. The only way to respond to a handwritten letter like this one is in kind . . . in writing. Or preferably in person."

Lilly took another sip of her wine. "Have to say I agree with your grandmother on this one."

"It wasn't a love letter, Grandmère," I said, feeling even more mortified as I scrambled to my feet. "He crossed out the word 'love,' didn't you see?"

"Yes, I did see that. Which means only, of course, that he is uncertain of the return of his affections, and is embarrassed to reveal too much. He is young. It is to be forgiven in this case."

"Or it could mean what it says." I couldn't remember ever having felt more wretched. "That he only likes me as a friend. Or that he used to."

Mia frowned. "Don't pay any attention to Grandmère, Olivia. It's fine to text Prince Khalil back, if that's what you want to do—"

Grandmère's jaw dropped. "Text him? TEXT HIM? Certainly not! When a man cares enough to expose his very soul in pen and ink, unless the woman finds him repulsive—which I am guessing you do not—it is the height of rudeness to respond using a mechanical device. Of course if you *don't* like the boy—"

Mia held up one finger, reminding everyone in the room that she was not only the current ruler of our country, but also a woman who had recently given birth to twins and wasn't going to put up with any nonsense from anyone, even her own grandmother.

"You're going to see Prince Khalil tomorrow night at your birthday ball," Mia reminded me. "He RSVP'd yes, and hasn't canceled. I had the Royal Genovian Press Office double check. So whatever you might believe he thinks of you, he's still coming here tomorrow night, so you can respond in person, like Grandmère said."

I felt engulfed in panic—but also a kind of excitement, too, at the same time. Prince Khalil was coming *here*, to the palace?

What on earth was I going to say to him when he got here?

Well, at the very least I could show him Carlos, my iguana, and how much he'd grown since Khalil had last been here, and I suppose I could show him the frog I'd seen in the gardens, the one I'd lied about being a Karpathos—

Wait. What was I thinking? He wasn't going to care about any of that.

He was going to want to know why I hadn't responded to his letter.

If he cared about me at all anymore, which was doubtful after I'd been so rude to him . . . and of course since he'd reignited his flame with the fiery-haired Princess Sophie Eugenie.

"But I think it's a bit late to be discussing any of this," Mia went on, "especially after you've had such a long journey. I think you'll feel better after a good night's rest."

"That is certainly true," Grandmère said. "I feel as if I'm developing a slight scratch in my throat. It's delightful to visit the mountains now and again, but only so that one can feel a better appreciation for the sea when one returns."

So we all went to bed . . . but not before Grandmère, as she was about to turn toward her own room— where her maid, Maxine, would be waiting with Grandmère's hot water bottle and bedtime tonic— said to me, "Don't worry about Prince Khalil, Olivia. If it turns out he does like this horrid other girl and not you, he's not worth having. Because that means he doesn't have a shred of common sense."

I shook my head. "This other girl isn't horrid, Grandmère. She's very nice, actually, from what I hear. And she's an excellent hockey goalie, even though our team beat hers."

She snorted.

"Never mind all that. You have skills that are just as valuable, and any boy, prince or not, who doesn't want you is an *imbecile*."

Then she slapped me on the behind and said, "Now go to bed. You know a woman must have eight hours of sleep a night to look her best in the morning. And I don't know about you, but I did NOT get a full eight hours of sleep one single night while I was in Stockerdörfl. I was up much too late every night, chasing the Duke of Marborough and his horrid little friend the marquis away from the hot tub, which for some reason they seemed intent on filling with bubble bath. Good night, *ma petite princesse.*"

Saturday, November 28
11:00 A.M.
MY BIRTHDAY
Royal Pool

When I woke up this morning (on my own. Francesca didn't wake me up, because it's my birthday, so for once I was allowed to sleep as late as I wanted to, because there's no school, no royal appearance, and no special event to attend today except my BIRTHDAY BALL TONIGHT) and went downstairs to eat breakfast, *no one was around.*

No one! In a palace full of people!

It took me a while to figure out where everyone

had gone. I had to ask the majordomo, who finally told me:

- Mia and Michael had taken the twins to their first postbirth checkup at the pediatrician.

- Dad, Helen, and Rocky were on some kind of secret mission (I assume to do with my birthday, hoping to surprise me, since the majordomo wouldn't give me any details. But I've already had the biggest surprise any girl could get in her life: finding out that her dad is actually the Prince of Genovia!).

- Lilly had gone off somewhere with Mia's bodyguard, Lars, because it's Lars's day off.

  This isn't unusual. Whenever Lilly is in town and Lars has a day off, the two of them go off somewhere. Nishi thinks they are having a love affair, but Nishi thinks that about everyone.

  I think it is more likely that Lars is showing Lilly the lovely Genovian countryside.

- And the rest of the palace staff was running around, trying to get everything ready for my party.

Fortunately Chef Bernard had recovered from his bout of La Grippe in time for my birthday, and had left some breakfast for me (my favorite, chocolate croissants). I took the plate and headed out to the pool, where I found Grandmère sunbathing in her pajamas.

"Hi, Grandmère," I said, sitting on a chaise longue beside her.

"Well, good morning, darling," she said, lowering her sunglasses so she could get a proper look at me. "Happy birthday."

"Thanks. Grandmère, why are you still dressed in your pajamas?"

"Oh, Dr. Khan was here and said that while I don't have La Grippe, I do have a slight cold—no doubt from having spent so many hours in the company of that odious young duke, who does not seem like the healthiest fellow—and advised that I rest and drink plenty of fluids before your ball tonight. Genovian sunshine always does me good after I've been away, so I'm absorbing some. And these are lounging pajamas, Olivia, not sleeping pajamas. I'm lounging. My question to you is, why are you not wearing your pajamas? It's your birthday. You could wear pajamas all day if you wanted to."

"Thanks, but I don't want to."

"Suit yourself. But I think the benefits of lounging will grow on you as you get older."

I put my plate of chocolate croissants aside so that Snowball couldn't get at them and stretched out on the chaise longue.

"Maybe," I said. "But the truth is, I'm a whole year older today, and I feel exactly the same as I did yesterday."

Grandmère sighed. "Get used to it. Aside from a more frequent desire to lounge, I don't feel a day older than I did when I was your age."

This caused me to sit up and stare at her in surprise. "Really? You still feel thirteen? But you've done so much with your life!"

"Yes, I have," Grandmère said, turning her face back toward the sun—though of course her skin was well shielded from its rays by an enormous floppy hat. "But that doesn't mean I *feel* any differently. When I was thirteen, I was certain I knew everything in the world there was to know."

"And?" I asked eagerly. "Did you?"

She laughed. Well, not so much laughed as cackled. "Oh, yes, my dear. *Absolutely*."

I sighed with envy.

I've only been thirteen for less than twelve hours (four if you count the fact that I was born at eight in the morning) and I feel like I know *less* than I did when I was twelve, thanks to Prince Khalil's letter.

Saturday, November 28
4:00 P.M.
Royal Genovian Bedroom

Olivia's Thirteenth Birthday Gift List
(Don't forget to write thank-you notes!):

Aunt Lilly gave me an official New York City
Statue of Liberty pen (because I'm always writing in
notebooks, she said) AND my very own giant
Toblerone chocolate bar.

(Later, I overheard her brother, Michael, accus-
ing her of having given me things she bought at a

JFK airport gift shop on her way to Genovia. Lilly said, "So what? She likes them, doesn't she?" which is true, so I don't see what the problem is.)

Michael and Mia got me my first pair of skis, including a gift certificate for ski boots (you can't buy ski boots for someone. They have to go to the store and try them on, to make sure they fit).

This is a very excellent present, considering I really like skiing. Although I've only done it once. Still, skiing is much more fun than salmon fishing in Iceland.

The twins got me a new iPod (because I dropped my last one in the waves at the beach), fully loaded with all my favorite singer-songwriters, as well as a box of hand-dipped Genovian truffles, with assorted flavors inside.

Rocky got me a gigantic purple bean-bag chair for my room, big enough to fit two adults, let alone kids.

I'm pretty sure he got me this because he likes coming into my room and hanging out, and this is what he'd like to sit in.

But that's okay. It's still cool.

Paolo got me the complete line of Principessa lip and nail colors (which is interesting because he designed it, so I know he got it for free) and said I was going to have to be extra careful now about my facial cleansing routine in order to avoid break-outs since I'm officially a teen. Thanks for the reminder!

Francesca got me a fancy alarm clock. I feel as if she is trying to say something with this gift—like that I'm old enough now not to need a wardrobe con-sultant to wake me. I hope this isn't true. I enjoy having Francesca wake me up. It is nice to see her bright mauve lipstick first thing every morning.

Serena bought me giant bags of the sweet and savory snacks from the train, because she says if I like sweet and savory so much, I should have them every day.

Serena just gets me.

Dad and Helen got me a sterling silver retractable table tennis net. It looks like a pen and fits in your pocket, but when you take it out and push a button—*voilà*! It's a standard-issue table tennis net that you can attach to just about any surface to turn that surface into a tennis table. All you need after that is a couple of paddles and a ball, and you're playing.

Dad also included a platinum charm bracelet with charms of paddles, balls, a pony that looks like Chrissy, a miniature poodle that looks like Snowball, a tiara, a pen, an artist's palette, and a diamond-encrusted outline of the country of Genovia, because Dad can't do anything small.

But that's why we love him.

Nishi got me the complete collection of my sister's

unauthorized biographies. "Don't tell her!" Nishi said. "I'm sure she won't want you to read them."

I have hidden them under my bed. I probably won't read them, since I know Mia wouldn't want me to. But I might sneak a peek at some of the Michael stuff later. Nishi says it's hilarious.

She still expects me to send a shirtless photo of Prince Khalil, smiling in front of a sunset, or I'll forever be a "bet squelcher." I have no idea how I'm supposed to capture this image.

I didn't tell her about Prince Khalil's letter. I don't know why. It just feels too . . . private, in a way.

Maybe I really *am* growing up.

The weirdest present I got is the one from Prince Gunther's parents, which they'd told me not to open until my birthday. It turns out *not* to be a key to Stockerdörfl:

It's a beautiful gold-link chain with a jewel-encrusted heart pendant hanging from it.

"Oh, my," Mia said when I opened the box at the table.

After I lounged around the pool for most of the

day, we all got together for a late birthday lunch in the garden, since we knew when everyone started arriving for my ball, we probably wouldn't be seeing much of each other.

Mia said she'd only be putting in a token appearance because of wanting to keep the babies away from any potential sources of La Grippe contagion. Grandmère said she was going to lock herself in her bedroom for the duration of the party. "I cannot face the Twelfth Duke of Marborough again so soon after having spent five hours on a train with him yesterday," she said. "I fear I will do him physical harm."

When Grandmère saw the neck- lace from Prince Gunther's par- ents, she said, "*Well.* You do seem to have made quite an impression on that boy's family. Are those *diamonds?*"

I looked more closely at the pendant. "Yes. I think so."

"Good heavens." Mia took

the necklace from me. "I don't know if it's all right for you to accept such an expensive gift from someone who is not a family member, Olivia. What do you think, Dad?"

Dad looked confused. "It's a necklace. The Lapsburg von Stubens like her. So what?"

Grandmère rolled her eyes. "The father is always the last to see."

Both Michael and my dad looked up at that. "See what?" they asked.

"That it's a little like a bribe," Mia said. "To date their son."

"WHAT!" I nearly dropped the necklace into my birthday cake (we were having two. One just for family, and another that would be brought out at my birthday ball, for guests. Chef Bernard had worked overtime to make both, and had apparently been driving the kitchen staff crazy to get them finished). "No! No, it's not! Prince Gunther doesn't think of me in that way!"

Mia, Grandmère, and even Helen and Lilly and one of the footmen looked at me with sympathetic expressions on their faces, while Michael, Rocky, and Dad just looked shocked.

"I think we'll put this away," Dad said, taking the necklace from Mia and slipping it into his pocket, "until you're a little older, Olivia."

"What?" I cried. "Why? I swear, Prince Gunther doesn't like me in that way!"

"You'll still have to write a thank-you note for it," Mia went on, gently rocking the babies.

"WHAT?" I said again. "What is happening?"

"Never mind, dear," Grandmère said. "Someday you'll understand. Until then, I have another necklace you can wear tonight. You can have it today as my birthday present to you."

And after lunch, Grandmère did give it to me—I'm wearing it now: a diamond pendant shaped like a heart, on a platinum chain, a little like the one in the movie *Titanic* (which Mia and I also watched together this summer), only not as big, of course.

"There," Grandmère said as she put it around my neck. "That looks beautiful—much better on you than it does on me at my age . . . though of course I think a woman can get away with wearing anything she wants at any age—except of course sleeveless leotards—so long as she wears it with confidence."

I fingered the diamond heart. It wasn't a pendant made of diamonds—it was a huge diamond cut into the shape of a heart.

"Thanks, Grandmère. Where did you get it?"

"Your grandfather gave it to me shortly before we were married, when there was a contretemps with a certain baron we both knew. It is better not to speak of it. Suffice it to say, your grandfather wanted to be assured of my affections, and he felt the quickest way to *my* heart was with a heart . . . a diamond one. Which is nonsense, of course. The quickest way to anyone's heart is by getting to know what is in their heart. Now, go and prepare for your party. I have the feeling it's going to be quite interesting."

I do, too. But probably not for the same reasons as Grandmère.

Sunday, November 29
2:00 A.M.
Royal Genovian Bedroom

This went from being the worst birthday I ever had to the best to the worst . . . to the best . . . to the . . .

I don't even know! Because it's still *happening*!

The only way I'm going to figure it out is if I write it down. Because then maybe my head will stop buzzing and my fingers will stop shaking and my heart will stop pounding . . .

Or not.

But more than anything what I felt all day today was super nervous to see Prince Khalil.

Which is silly, because I'd never been nervous to see him before. Why now, just because he'd written me a letter saying he thought I was the coolest girl he'd ever met and wanted to get to know me better?

Well. I guess I know why. I could fool the people around me, but I couldn't fool myself:

Because I liked him, too. And not as a friend, either. Why else had I gotten so upset when I'd learned that he'd sent me that letter, and I hadn't seen it for a whole week, and had left him hanging with no reply?

If I didn't like him—*really* like him—I wouldn't have cared.

No, Luisa had been right all along—and that was another reason I was so mad at her:

I had a crush on Prince Khalil.

And finding out that he liked me back—maybe even had a crush on me, too—was the best birthday present I could have ever had.

If he still liked me.

There was only one way to find out—not including texting him to ask, which I had to agree with

Grandmère seemed like a cheesy, nonprincessy thing to do. Ten-year-old girls slip boys notes—or texts—asking if he likes her.

Thirteen-year-old princesses ask in person.

So that's what I was going to do.

I was so nervous, I thought I might actually throw up all the Toblerone and sweet and savory snacks I'd eaten all day.

Paolo was still screwing around with my hair when guests started arriving for the ball. But it was worth it, because when he was done, he and Francesca looked at me and said, *"Bellissima!"*

I know they weren't lying to make me feel better. I did look beautiful, and it is not bragging to say that. Partly it was the way he'd done my hair—in curly tendrils on top of my head—and partly it was the dress—made by my cousin Sebastiano. It was purple (my favorite color), with crystals on top and a full length, floaty skirt on the bottom, with more crystals on the bottom.

I really did look *bellissima.*

When I walked out into the hallway where Dad

was waiting, checking his watch and shouting at the door every two minutes ("Olivia, I know you don't care, but I do actually want to walk you down the stairs while you are still thirteen!"), he agreed.

"Now THAT was worth waiting for," he said.

"Thanks, Dad," I said. "You look good, too."

He *did*, too, with his shiny bald head and black tuxedo jacket with tails. He gave me his arm and led me proudly to the Grand Royal Staircase, where Helen, Mia, Michael, Lilly, Rocky, and even Grandmère (in a lavender evening gown, with Rommel wearing a matching feather boa) were all waiting.

"Oh, Olivia, you look beautiful," Mia said, while

Michael took about a million photos with his new computer watch.

I tried to get them to stop fussing, since I could see everyone in the Great Hall down below, looking up at me. I'm grateful to have a family (at last) that loves me.

But sometimes they still totally embarrass me.

"Turn to the left," Lilly said, snapping a few of her own photos. "The portrait of that weird guy in the suit of armor is behind you."

"Oh, yes," Grandmère said, glancing at Lilly's screen. "Prince Reginald. Such an unfortunate chin. Phillipe, do steer her a little to the left."

"No," I said, through gritted teeth. "It's my party. We're going now."

I couldn't tell if Prince Khalil was in that crowd below—there were too many young men wearing tuxedoes to tell them apart from the top of the staircase.

But as Dad led me down the Grand Royal Staircase, I said a quick little prayer that he'd shown up. Just because he'd RSVP'd didn't mean anything. Lots of people RSVP these days—Chef Bernard is always complaining—and then don't show up (or don't RSVP, and do show up), leaving the kitchen with an uneven plate count.

Down Dad and I went, to where everyone was waiting.

"I love your dress," gushed all the girls (well, most of them. Luisa made a point of saying, "Oh, is that another Sebastiano? It figures.").

"Where's the food?" asked all the boys (not Prince Khalil. I did not see him. Yet).

There was plenty of food. Chef Bernard need not have worried. He had totally outdone himself and made all my favorites (despite Grandmère's objections that there was nothing "healthy" on the menu), including: cheeseburger sliders; multiple types of pizza; Genovian fruit, veggie, tofu (for the vegans), and cheese platters; roll-ups and spirals; chicken wings; cones of fries; nachos; popcorn with every imaginable topping; an ice-cream sundae bar; and of course, birthday cake and a chocolate fountain with everything from marshmallows to miniature cheese-cakes to dip in it (I really hoped Prince Khalil noticed the last bit).

Soon people were gorging themselves and dancing by the pool and in the ballroom (we'd opened all the French doors so you could wander in and out).

Dad and Helen's surprise turned out to be none other than Boris P and his band. The place they'd disappeared to with Rocky in the morning was the Genovian airport, where they'd met Boris, his band, and his girlfriend, Tina Hakim Baba. They'd flown in on Boris P's private plane.

And yes, I *know* he's a worldwide superstar, and I should be very grateful and honored that he's come to Genovia TWICE in the past year to play at the palace.

But he's not MY favorite. I really should let people know that I'm not a Borette.

But whatever. Victorine (and Marguerite, who'd recovered enough from La Grippe to be officially noncontagious and attend the ball) and everyone else was over the MOON when they found out Boris P was the musical entertainment.

And Mia was excited to have her friend Tina Hakim Baba visiting. Tina was ecstatic to see the babies, who really are looking cuter and cuter every day, even if the public (and Grandmère) aren't completely thrilled with their names (most people seem to like Elizabeth, but a national poll found that 68 percent think that "Prince Frank" isn't very royal).

"Prince Francesco I could understand," I overheard Grandmère saying. "Even Prince Francis would be passable. But Frank? Prince *Frank*? I've never heard a less royal name in all my life."

Fortunately Rocky was busy at the chocolate fountain when Grandmère said this.

Anyway, I did not mean to look as if I weren't enjoying myself at my own party. If I did, it wasn't because of Grandmère's complaining . . . and it definitely wasn't because of Boris P.

It was because I finally spied Prince Khalil through the throng of people in the ballroom—I'd invited everyone who attends the Royal Genovian

Academy, practically, except the kindergartners and first graders, because let's face it, I did not want a bunch of babies at my party—and he did not come near me.

At all.

Who could blame him, really? If I had sent a letter like that to him, and HE had not responded in a week, I would not have come near him, either. I would probably not even have come to his party.

So it was generous of him even to have shown up. Why shouldn't he have hung out with Tots and the duke and those guys over by the pool table in the billiard room?

I probably would have done the same thing.

So maybe I was *momentarily* looking a little down at one point, and that is why Prince Gunther approached me and yelled (you had to yell because Boris P was playing his new hit single "The Love in Your Eyes," so loudly), "Princess Olivia. Is everything all right?"

"Everything is fine," I said (yelled). "How are you?"

"I am not so fine," Prince Gunther said. "As you know, Lady Luisa and I broke up."

"Yes," I said. "I know. I'm sorry."

"Yes." Prince Gunther pointed at his red cummerbund. "I still wear Claudio, though. She can kill my heart, but she cannot kill my love for fashion."

"Oh," I said. I could sense that Prince Gunther had something he really wanted to say to me, but it was so loud in the ballroom, where Boris P and his band were playing, that I could barely hear a thing other than their music.

"Gunther," I said, even though a part of me really didn't want to. "Do you want to—"

"Dance? Yes, very much! We make good dance partners, remember?"

"No. I meant go somewhere less noisy."

"Yes! This I want to do, too."

So we stepped out into the royal gardens, which wasn't much quieter than inside, because of course there were speakers to amplify the music. But at least there was *slightly* less noise.

I found a nice spot near the pool—close to where

Grandmère and I had been in the morning—and sat down, though I first had to kick a few purple and white balloons out of the way.

"This is perfect," Prince Gunther said, looking around admiringly at the garlands of flowers the palace staff had spent all afternoon stringing up. "Very romantic!"

"Uh," I said. "Well, I guess you could call it that. . . . Look, Gunther, about my cousin. I don't think you should feel too badly about her. I don't know if you two were meant to—"

"Oh," he said, looking at my throat. "You are not wearing my necklace."

I put my hand to my chest. Oops. "Oh. No. I'm not."

He frowned. "You did not like it?"

"No, Prince Gunther, I do like it. Very much. I'm writing to thank your parents, in fact, because it was such a thoughtful, generous gift. But my dad thought it was maybe a little *too* generous, and I should wait to wear it when I'm older."

"Too generous?" Prince Gunther looked confused.

There was an almost full moon, so I could see him pretty well, especially with the bright blue glow from the pool and all the party globes the palace staff had hung from the palm trees. "How can a gift be *too* generous?"

"Well," I said.

This was starting to feel uncomfortable, and I regretted my decision to leave the ballroom. There weren't as many people outside, and the ones who were there were the older high school students at the RGA, many of whom were clustered in exactly the things Madame Alain most despised—friend groups— and were paying no attention whatsoever to me and Prince Gunther.

"You see," I began, trying to explain to Prince Gunther what I meant, which was difficult, since I didn't even know what I meant, or why exactly my dad had taken the necklace away, "it's a heart necklace, made of gold and diamonds—"

"So is the one you are wearing," he said. "Only that one is silver."

"Platinum," I said. "Not that it matters. But this

one was a gift from my grandmother, not a boy to whom I'm not related—"

"But we *could* be related."

I stared at him. "No, Prince Gunther," I said. "We could not. The Lapsburg von Stubens and the Renaldos are not related in any way, that I know of . . ."

"No," he said, taking my hand. "I mean if we get married."

Oh no! A million alarm bells went off in my head. No, no, no, no! This could not be happening. Not on my birthday. Not on *any* day. This was never supposed to happen.

Then again, how could I have been so stupid not to have seen it? Prince Gunther had already told me once before that he liked me.

But that had been so long ago! Sixth grade, a million years ago.

Of course, sixth grade was not a million years ago. It only *felt* that way. It was technically only six months ago.

But that was long enough.

"No, Prince Gunther," I said, gently withdrawing my hand from his. "That is not going to happen."

"It could," he said eagerly. "Once we've graduated from college, of course. I plan to study computer engineering. I would like to design my own video games."

"That's great," I said. "But that's a long time from now. And you're only just getting out of a long-term relationship. So I think you need to take some time to play the field before you decide who to date next, let alone marry."

I had no idea what I was talking about, but this was the kind of stuff I heard Mia's friends talking about all the time, so I thought it sounded good.

It seemed to sound good to Prince Gunther, too, since he said, "Hmmm. Well, maybe that is true."

"I know it is," I said. "You said yourself that Lady Luisa broke your heart. It takes time for that kind of wound to heal, and the only way for that to happen is for you to really get to know yourself. Who is Prince Gunther Lapsburg von Stuben?"

Prince Gunther looked toward the stars. "That is something I often ask myself."

"I'm sure you do. But it's a question only you can answer. And when you do, maybe you'll want to give that heart necklace to some other girl."

Prince Gunther glanced away from the stars and back at me. "Oh, Princess Olivia," he said. "That will never happen."

"Okay," I said. "Well, I think you're wrong. But I'll hold on to it for you in the meantime, even though I really don't think I'm the right girl for it . . . or for you."

He sighed. "I thought this might happen. But thank you for being so kind about it, Princess Olivia." He gave a sigh, then stood up to go. "You will always be the princess of my heart."

Then he winked, put his hands into his pockets, and shuffled away, whistling a little tune. As I sat staring after him, I saw Nadia and Princess Komiko bounce toward him, eager—as always—to cheer him up. They dragged him into the ballroom, and began to dance to Boris P's other new hit, "You Light Me Up."

I looked down at the spot where he'd been sitting. Oh my goodness! Had that really just happened?

I got my answer more quickly than expected. It turned out there'd been a witness: my cousin Luisa. She'd been spying on me.

"Ha! I heard all that. And you were so worried about my breaking Prince Gunther's heart."

Luisa came strolling up, a plastic cup of fruit punch in her hand. (I know it's tacky to use plastic cups, but since the babies were born, Michael won't allow the use of glass receptacles by the pool, since someone might break them and then the babies could cut their tiny feet when they learn how to walk.)

"Luisa," I said grumpily, "go away."

"But I guess I didn't break Prince Gunther's heart, did I?" Luisa asked. "Not if he was so willing to give it to you a day later!"

"You're wrong," I said, glaring at her. She was wearing a red Claudio evening gown, just as she'd said she would in her note to me, so many days ago. "You really hurt his feelings."

"Oh, right." She narrowed her eyes on me. "He's soooo sad. So sad he just asked you to marry him!"

I felt myself blush. "That was just Gunther. You know how he—"

"Ha!" She took a sip of punch. "Don't worry about it. Do you think I'm jealous? I'm not. I'm glad, actually. He deserves someone nice. Nicer than me, anyway."

I sighed. "You *are* nice, Luisa. Or you could be, if you'd just try."

"But being mean is so fun." She wiggled her eyebrows at me. "I know you know that. And if you weren't such a stick-in-the-mud, you could have fun being mean along with me."

"No," I said. "Do you know what all of this is about, Luisa?" I waved my arms to indicate the pool, the gardens, the party, the palace. "I mean being royal, and having good manners. What it's really, *really* all about?"

"Uh . . . letting people walk all over you?"

"No. It's about putting yourself in the other person's shoes and trying to think how *you*'d want to be treated if you were in their place, and then treating them that way. It's called *empathy*. You should look it up sometime."

"I know what empathy means," Luisa said acidly. "That's why I let Prince Gunther break up with me."

I rolled my eyes at this. "Oh, *come on*, Luisa. You did not *let* Prince Gunther break up with you. He dumped you fair and square when he finally saw you with the duke."

"I *let* him see me with the duke," Luisa said, pointing at me. "Because you told me what I was doing to him was unfair. Despite what you may think, Stick, I *did* care about Prince Gunther's feelings, and I realized I didn't want him to get hurt any more than I'd already hurt him. So I let him go, just like you asked me to."

I pointed back at her. "No," I said. "That's not what I—"

"Oh, maybe I didn't do it the way *you* would have done it, but I do have empathy—and manners—see?"

She dropped her arm. "So now, if you'll excuse me, Your Very Royal Highness, I have to go. The duke is waiting for me. We're going to try to unplug Boris P's amplifiers and make everyone stop dancing and freak out. Happy birthday!"

"Thanks," I called to her as she walked away, though I didn't actually feel very grateful to her. I felt like giving her a swift kick in the pants (or the back of her ball gown).

But one thing you can't change, unlike your hair or your shoes, is other people. Only they can do that.

Sadly, they almost never do.

But there's always hope.

"Princess Olivia?"

What now? I thought. What could possibly go wrong next?

So I turned around . . .

. . . and there was Prince Khalil.

My heart did a flip in my chest. I swear, it was like when one of the figure skaters at the Royal School Winter Games flipped over backward on the ice. Only it happened right inside of my chest.

I have no idea if it landed right side up again. I could have an upside-down heart now, for all I know. It would explain a *lot*.

I could barely breathe, Prince Khalil looked so nice standing there in the steam coming off the pool (because it was kind of cold outside, but the water in the pool is heated), with his white shirt collar open at the neck and his black tie untied and his dark eyes so bright and shiny.

"Oh," I managed to say. Don't ask me how. "Hi. I didn't see you there."

Most brilliant thing in the world to say. *Hi. I didn't see you there.* Obviously.

"Yes," he said, coming closer. "Well, you've been very busy all night. Everyone's wanted to wish you a happy birthday."

I looked at a star directly above his head and wished very hard that he had not overheard my conversations with either Prince Gunther or Lady Luisa.

"Yes," I said. "Well, that's what happens at birthday parties. Listen, Prince Khalil. I just wanted to say that I got your—"

"Here," he interrupted, and thrust something into my fingers. "This is for you."

I looked down. In my hand was a small, somewhat tattered velvet box.

"Oh," I said, surprised and embarrassed at the same time. "Prince Khalil . . . you didn't have to get me a gift. It said on the invitation—"

"'The gift of your presence is present enough,'" he said with a laugh. "I know. But I saw this, and I thought you'd like it. Open it."

Completely embarrassed now—but at least I know WHY I'm always embarrassed when I'm around him (because I really, really like him)—I sat back down on the chaise longue and opened the velvet box.

Inside was the smallest little painting I've ever seen, on very old parchment paper, of some animals sitting around a lake. It was so exquisitely and brilliantly painted, each color looked like it had been mixed with crushed jewels before it had been spread onto the tiny canvas.

"Oooh," I exclaimed, afraid to touch it—or even breathe—because it was so small and beautiful, like the twins had become, now that they'd gotten over the trauma of being born.

"Do you know what it is?" Prince Khalil asked, sitting down beside me. In fact, he nudged me over, so that I'd make room for him, not exactly something a boy who was madly in love with someone would do . . .

. . . unless of course he felt so comfortable with the girl, and he was so excited about the subject they were discussing, he didn't realize he'd done it.

"No," I said, looking only at him, not the painting.

"It's called a Persian miniature," he said. "It's from my country. Very few of them exist anymore, at least outside of museums, because of my uncle." His face clouded over as he referred to the man who was systematically destroying his beloved homeland. "He doesn't like art, so he's demolishing every piece he finds."

I couldn't help letting out a little gasp. How could anyone want to purposely destroy something so beautiful?

"This is one we managed to get out before he discovered it," Prince Khalil went on. "It was painted many centuries ago. When I saw it, I thought of you, because the animals look like the ones you draw."

"Prince Khalil," I said, my heart not flipping over anymore. Now it had swollen to five times—maybe ten times—the size of the country of Genovia. "Thank you so much for thinking of me. But I can't keep this." It killed me to return it to him, but I thought of what Mia had said about Prince Gunther's gift, and I knew I had to. "It's far too valuable. I could never—"

"Oh, no," he interrupted, looking alarmed as I tried to thrust the tiny painting back into his hands. "You *must* keep it. You're the only person I know who'll appreciate it, and who'll take proper care of it. Because you're the only one who knows its true worth."

"Yes," I said. "Of course I do. But—"

He gently pushed the picture back into my hands. "This is a piece of my country's history—maybe the only piece left, if my uncle has his way. You'll take good care of it, the way you take good care of all the things you love. You understand about family. You understand about not hurting things, even things other people consider pests, like iguanas."

"Well," I said reluctantly. "Yes. But this—"

Everything he'd pointed out was true, of course. But it was such an enormous responsibility, I didn't know what to say. I held the tiny painting to my heart—carefully, so as not to crush it.

"Prince Khalil," I said, "thank you for entrusting this to me. I love it, and of course I'll make sure it's well cared for. Maybe . . . maybe I could put it in the museum here in the palace. We have lots of precious things there that other countries have entrusted into our care. And that way, other people can see and appreciate it, too, and there'll always be a piece of your country's history alive somewhere."

His dark eyes glittered in the moonlight. "Yes," he said. "I think that would be all right." Then he smiled. "I think that would be excellent, actually."

"Good," I said. Then, before I could stop myself, I added, "And about your letter. I want you to know that I only got it last night. It was lost in all the confusion when my sister's babies were born, with all the other letters that arrived earlier in the week, so I only just got a chance to read it—"

The light in his ink-dark eyes disappeared, and his eyebrows darted upward.

"Oh," he said. "So *that's* what happened! I wondered. When you never mentioned it, I thought . . . well, I thought maybe, since I always see you hanging around Prince Gunther . . ."

His voice trailed off, but I knew exactly what he meant.

I flung a hand to my face, mortified. "Oh, no! I mean, I do like Prince Gunther, but only as a friend. Not that I don't like you as a friend, too, but . . ."

Oh, this was terrible. I was only making things worse.

I put my hand on his.

"What I meant to say was, the answer is yes—if it's not too late. Yes, I would like to go have ice cream with you, or coffee, sometime." I said it all in a rush, so I would be sure to get it out correctly. "Well, I'd prefer ice cream, but anything would be great. Anytime. Right now, if you want."

He looked happier than I had ever seen him . . . happier than when the RGA had won the Royal School Winter Games, even.

"Great," Prince Khalil said, squeezing my hand in his. "Let's go!"

He pulled me up from the chaise longue.

"What?" I said with a disbelieving laugh. "Really?"

"Why not?" he asked. "You said anytime. Unless . . ." Then he looked around, and his smile faded. "Oh, right. It's your birthday party. You probably want to stay."

"No." I shook my head. "I don't! Do you want to know a secret?"

"Of course!"

"I hate Boris P."

His smile lit up the entire pool area. "I do, too!"

So we left. I left my own birthday party!

It's crazy, but it's true. It wasn't even hard. I asked my dad if it was okay, and at first he said, "No, absolutely not."

But Helen overheard and said, "Phillipe, remember how you told me to let you know when you were being stubborn and unreasonable?"

So Dad agreed to give us the bulletproof limo (only if we took Serena, too, and got the Royal Genovian Guard to do a precheck on the closest ice-cream shop, which of course was open late. It's Genovia on a Saturday night!).

So we rode down there—after I gave the painting to the chief of the Royal Genovian Guard for safekeeping; I knew he would make sure it stayed safe while I was gone—and ordered two cones. I got mint chocolate chip, and Prince Khalil got pralines and cream.

Then we sat on the seawall and looked out across the ocean, and talked about Persian miniatures, and Prince Khalil's home country, and Genovia, and New Jersey, and Prince Gunther, and Princess Sophie Eugenie (with whom he was *not* texting during the train ride home. He was texting back and forth with his mother, who loves to text, and loves heart emojis even more), and my pet iguana, Carlos, and wildlife illustration, and how much we hate Boris P's music.

And before I knew it, it was midnight, and Serena said she needed to get me back, and we dropped Prince Khalil off at the apartment building where he lives with his mom and dad. . . .

But not before I got a selfie of us sitting on the seawall in the moonlight, eating our ice-cream cones, our shoulders touching and our feet dangling above the waves. I told him I needed to send it to my friend Nishi.

"I lost a bet," I explained.

"Okay," he said, giving me a bewildered smile.

OlivGrace >

Sorry, Nishi, but I guess I'm a bet squelcher after all, because this is the only picture of Prince Khalil you're going to get!
XOXO Olivia

And now I'm starting to think that I was 100 percent wrong this morning when I told Grandmère that being thirteen feels exactly the same as being twelve.

Thirteen is *completely* different—and *so much better*—than being twelve.

Uh-oh. Nishi just got the photo I sent her, and is texting me back:

< NishiGirl

TELL ME EVERYTHING!!!!!!

But you know what? I'm not going to. Because some things are meant to be private. 😉

MEG CABOT

You illustrated the From the Notebooks of a Middle School Princess series yourself. What was your favorite thing to draw?
The royal crown! Princess Olivia gets to dress up in all sorts of royal clothes and jewels, and my favorite part is always designing her clothes and tiaras.

Olivia's school goes to the Royal School Winter Games. Were you athletic as a kid? If so, what sports/events did you compete in?
I was on my local Girl's Club softball team. We were terrible because most of us were only interested in hitting the ball, not catching or throwing it. We were the worst in the whole league, but we didn't care. Our coaches despaired of us.

What book is on your nightstand now?
Right now I'm reading a scary nonfiction book about how the FBI uses forensic science to catch criminals. It's what Netflix based their new series *Mindhunter* on! I think it's fun to scare yourself sometimes.

If you could go anywhere in the world, where would you go and what would you do?
I would go to Monaco, the royal principality on which Genovia is based! I was there once before, but I was only seven so I don't remember it very well. I want to see how well my memory measures up to the real thing. I'd tour the prince's castle and go to the beach like Olivia!

Prince Khalil impresses Grandmère (and Olivia!) with his ability to rap Tupac on the spot. Are there any musicians who you love and have memorized?
I love Tupac! But I love music from all genres, including rap, hip-hop, musical theater, classical, country western, and rock.

What is your favorite food? Are there any foods you won't eat?
I love pizza! However, I was diagnosed with celiac disease, which means I'm allergic to gluten (in wheat flour), so now I can only eat gluten-free. It stinks, but I like to concentrate on the positive: There are a lot more foods out there that I CAN eat than I can't!

Olivia had a hard time admitting that she had a crush on Prince Khalil. Do you remember who your first crush was?
Of course I remember my first crush! It was in the fifth grade, and it was a boy who liked snakes, just like Prince Khalil! I couldn't believe I ended up liking him, because I hated snakes! But in the end, he taught me that snakes weren't so bad. And we ended up holding hands at the school field trip to Western Skateland Roller Rink! I thought my face would break in two from smiling so hard. Then of course he moved to Wisconsin.

Both Khalil and Gunther tried to give Olivia great gifts for her birthday. What was the best gift you've ever received?

The best gift I ever received was my cat, who is a rescue from the ASPCA. She sleeps with me every night—in fact, she's sleeping on me right now, making this hard to type!

Olivia is very excited to become an aunt. Do you have any nieces or nephews?

I have thirteen nieces and nephews!! They range in ages from ten to twenty-six. They're a handful! Two of my nieces are rodeo barrel racing champions in their age brackets.

Do you have any advice for aspiring illustrators (wildlife or otherwise)?

Yes! Practice drawing every chance you get. Even people who've never drawn before can get good if they practice. The more you practice, the better you'll be!

Coronations, princely boyfriends, and royal babysitting duties. . . . When you're a princess of Genovia, nothing is simple.

Keep reading for an excerpt.

Monday, December 28
11:30 A.M.
Royal Pool

It's three days before my sister's royal coronation . . . the first coronation of a female ruler in Genovia in *two centuries*!

I should be having fun—especially since it's winter break, my best friend, Nishi, is visiting from America, and I get to be *in* the coronation ceremony.

But instead I'm being forced to entertain my snobby cousin Lady Luisa Ferrari because her grandmother, the baroness, is in Biarritz with her new gentleman friend.

"I'm bored," Luisa keeps saying.

"*You're* the one who said you wanted to work on your tan," I remind her. We're stretched out in the winter sun on chaise longues next to the pool, which is heated. But still.

"How can you be bored staying in a *royal palace*?" Nishi wants to know. She doesn't mind hanging by the pool, because even though it's only seventy degrees in Genovia right now, it's thirty-five and snowing in New Jersey, where Nishi's visiting from. "They have *everything* here: tennis courts, horseback riding, sailing, mani-pedis, a state-of-the-art home theater, all the food you can eat, prepared by a *five-star* chef—"

"Yes, but hello." Luisa holds up her phone. "The cell service? Horrible."

"What do you expect from a building that was constructed in medieval times?" I ask. "The walls had to be made three feet thick in order to keep out invading marauders."

"Yes, but now they're keeping out my cell phone service provider." Lady Luisa adjusts her floppy hat.

She wants to tan on her body, not her face. "It's no wonder the duke hasn't been able to reach me."

The duke. That's all Luisa ever talks about, her boyfriend, the Duke of Marborough.

I have a boyfriend, too—well, a friend-who-is-a-boy—but I don't talk about him all the time.

And I highly doubt that the reason Luisa hasn't heard from her boyfriend is because of the palace's thick walls. More likely it's because they're in another one of their fights. All Luisa and the duke ever do is fight, usually over the duke's refusal to do anything except play video games. Which would be all right if Luisa played video games, too, but she doesn't.

"You know, Luisa," I can't help pointing out, "you're living through one of the most momentous occasions in Genovian history. My sister's coronation on Thursday is going to be attended by over two hundred heads of state and televised worldwide—"

"Oh my God, I know," Luisa says with a yawn. "You've only mentioned it a million times. Could you please pass me the sunscreen?"

It's not really my cousin's fault that she's so rude. She actually has a pretty rough home life. Her parents are getting divorced and, according to my friend Princess Komiko, her mom and dad are fighting over who *isn't* going to get custody of Lady Luisa.

That's why Luisa lives with her grandmother in the first place, a grandmother who is always jetting off to places like Biarritz with new gentlemen friends.

"I don't understand why your sister even has to have a coronation ceremony, Olivia," Nishi says. "Isn't she already a princess?"

It's natural that Nishi would be confused about this, since she's from the US and hasn't been getting the endless lessons on the coronation that we have here in Genovia, both in school and on the nightly news.

"Of course she's already a princess," I say. "We both are, since our dad is a prince. But Dad is abdicating—which means giving up the crown—so that he can spend more time with me and Rocky. So on Thursday, at the coronation, Mia will formally take over the throne from my dad."

"Oh." Nishi adjusts her sunglasses. "But then why isn't she becoming a queen?"

I sigh. Royal life is complicated.

"Because Genovia is a principality," I explain, "which means it's ruled by either a prince or a princess, not a king or a queen."

"Um, technically, it's not ruled by either," Luisa says in a waspish voice. "Genovians have a prime minister. The royal family doesn't actually make any laws. Their role is only symbolic. So it's not like Princess Mia will actually ever *do* anything once she's crowned."

I suck in my breath, shocked.

But before I can tell Lady Luisa how rude she's

being, Rocky, my little stepbrother, comes bursting into the royal gardens, running at full speed, my miniature poodle, Snowball, barking at his heels.

"Olivia!" he shrieks. "They're here! They're finally here!"

"Good grief," Luisa says, lowering her sunglasses to get a better look at him. "What's *his* problem?"

What's yours? I want to ask her, even though I already know.

"What's here, Rocky?" I ask him instead, when he skids to a stop in front of us.

"The Robe of State," he pants. "And the royal crown!"

No more hanging out at the pool with my rude cousin for me! I've got a crown to inspect.

Monday, December 28
1:30 P.M.
Royal Sitting Room

I knew something was going to go wrong—something besides my having to entertain my awful cousin Lady Luisa all day (and night), I mean. It seems like my family can never have an ordinary, universally televised state function without it turning into a disaster.

And now it looks as if the coronation will be no exception.

Normally the royal crown is in a bulletproof glass case in the palace museum with all the other crown jewels.

But because my sister, Mia, will be wearing it later this week for the coronation, it was sent out for cleaning.

Now it's back and has been brought upstairs to our living quarters so that Paolo, the royal beauty stylist, can figure out which of Mia's hairdos will best keep it in place.

We were all standing around admiring it . . . and trying it on, even though the royal crown isn't supposed to be worn by anyone except the reigning monarch.

But Mia said it was okay, because when will we ever have another chance to try on the *actual royal crown of Genovia*?

MEG CABOT is the #1 *New York Times*–bestselling author of the beloved and critically acclaimed Princess Diaries books, which were made into wildly popular Disney movies of the same name. There have been over 25 million copies of Meg's books for both adults and teens/tweens sold in 38 countries. Her last name rhymes with habit, as in "her books can be habit-forming." She currently lives in Key West, Florida, with her husband and various cats.

megcabot.com
MiddleSchoolPrincessBooks.com

The Royal Genovian Family Tree

By Olivia Grace

HRH Rosagund
(1st Princess of Genovia)

HRH Clarisse Grimaldi Renaldo
(Dowager Princess of Genovia,
AKA Grandmère)

HRH Artur Gerard Christoff
Phillipe Grimaldi Renaldo
(71st Prince of Genovia,
AKA Grandpère)

Lady Belle Beauty of Windenham
(Snowball's Mom)

*Note: HRH stands for
Her (or His) Royal Highness